CW00517690

DESPICABLE

RORY MILES

dedication

To Chad—no. You know what?

F**K Chad.

AUTHOR'S NOTE

Hey! This is a fun and spicy read! Bellatrix is a wild child, and I think you'll love her men! This book does have MM, so if you're not into that, this book probably isn't for you.

Happy reading :D.

Copyright © 2021 by Rory Miles

All rights reserved.

Reproducing this book without permission from the author or the publisher is an infringement of its copyright. This book is a work of fiction. The character names, names of places, and incidents are products of the author's imagination and are not to be construed as real or used without the author's authorization. Any resemblance to any actual events or persons, living or dead, locale or organizations is entirely coincidental.

Cover by: Paradise Cover Design

❀ Created with Vellum

one

BELLATRIX

Before we begin, there's something you need to know.

I'm not a good girl, not even close. I'm not always polite. I'm not a flower. I'm definitely not a virgin. I'm bad. I'm brash. I'm jagged glass, with specks of blood. And I like sex.

A lot.

Not like a nymphomaniac, but there's something about the way two strangers can lock gazes from opposite sides of a dark club and be drawn to each other. Like moths to a flame, and said flame is filthy, dirty, hot sex.

I stare into the stranger's eyes, seeing an instant flare of desire flash across his face when the stage lights turn white and brush over his olive colored skin. He's with his friends who are all laughing and staring out at the dancing women, but he doesn't spare any of them a glance. I tip my head to the side ever so slightly and arch an eyebrow.

Like I said, the pull of sexual tension between two random strangers can be magnetic, and I've never been one to deny the feeling. The rush which comes with chance encounters isn't half bad either.

Anyway, the reason you need to know all of this is so you understand the expression on my face when my sister says, "I wonder if I'll find *him*. Moons, can you imagine? True love!" Belladonna squeals.

Cue the look.

One eyebrow raised, the other drawn down, lips quirked to the side in a weird grimace, and head pulled back.

"Oh, don't give me that look, *Bellatrix*."

Uh-oh. She's using my full name. Yeah, I know, my parents got a bit out of hand with the nearly matching names, but I've lived with it my whole life.

"A whole new pack means a whole new group of men who might just be our fated mates," my sister says like there is hope for me yet.

"Bella, I'm twenty-seven. Twenty. Seven. You know the chances of finding a fated mate goes down astronomically the older you get. Hell, I'll be lucky if I find a regular mate given my age."

Not that I want to find either. I quite enjoy my nights of debauchery and reveling in the tension that comes with lust and then leaving them before things get too serious.

Before I can get hurt.

Trust me, it's much safer this way. A lot more fun too.

"Trix," she groans. "Not this again."

I roll my eyes and sip on my dirty martini, eyeing the wall of muscle which takes the spot a few seats away from us to order a drink. I knew he'd come over the minute we made eye contact from across the dance floor. His dark gray eyes slide over me like a cool caress, eliciting a slight shiver. I can practically see his dick growing hard by the way he's staring at me, and the thought of me making him erect has heat pooling low in my belly.

Biting my cheek, I focus on my sister, ignoring his lustful gaze.

The trick is to snare them, then play hard to get for a little while. Things like this always go the same way. We both want one thing, but he needs a little bit of a chase to truly get into it, and I take pride in being memorable. Especially with the tall, muscled ones. There's nothing quite as satisfying as making the sexy ones beg for more. If I weren't a wolf, I'd be a succubus for sure.

Clearing my throat, I set the martini down. "Yes, this. Are you going to sit there and tell me I'm wrong?"

Pinning her with my best squinting glare, I wait for her to try and deny it. She doesn't. Probably because she knows I'm right. Fated mates are every young wolf's dream. When I was little, I used to imagine my fated mate as some prince who would swoop in and save me from my normal but boring childhood. Some majestic being who would make me swoon and keep me safe inside a mystical castle as we built a beautiful family.

Spoiler alert: He never came.

Years passed and I turned eighteen. For a while there, during every full moon, I hoped I'd run into him. I would run for miles in my wolf form, passing dozens of wolves in our pack lands only to find he wasn't there. I watched one by one as all of my friends found a fated mate.

The moon-blessed bond between two wolves that's so powerful it can bring an alpha wolf to his knees for his female counterpart. If they didn't find a fated by around twenty-four, most settled with a regular mate. There's still a bond with a regular mate, but it's not moon-blessed, not destined to be.

Bella wrinkles her nose. "Don't be so pessimistic, Trix. He's out there." Her eyes fill with shining hope for what might be.

Of course she thinks so. I look at my drink so I don't roll my eyes again at her dramatics.

"You're probably right," I say softly, not wanting to hurt her.

She's six years younger than me, and I remember being as in love with the idea of fated love as she is.

As it turns out, I'm destined to be single. The universe is

cruel. It's fine. I've come to terms with it, and I rather like the trouble I find on my own. Especially when the biceps are so defined and the hair is so perfectly styled. My eyes slip back to the curious stranger, and I bite my bottom lip and bat my eyelashes before looking away again.

He's already hooked, but what's a little more suspense on his part? He'll come way harder if he thinks he was the one who snared me.

Bella notices my straying attention and huffs. "Seriously?"

Shrugging, I take a healthy drink. "We're moving. This is our last night out. Don't you want to have a little fun? Besides, Mallory is over there screeching your name, and I know you're dying to go be with your bestie. You don't have to hang out with me because you feel sorry for me."

The guy shoots me another look, and I quirk the corner of my lip before glancing at my nearly empty drink. He's a goner. He's so human it hurts, but it's a good thing he is because he can't hear our conversation. Not with the music blaring this loud.

Nothing kills the mood faster than fated mate talk.

"Are you sure you're all right? I don't want to bail on you." Bella finally gives in and glances at Mallory, who is dancing with a few other girls. They all wave my sister over.

"Oh, don't you worry about me. I think I'll have company soon enough." I slide my glass to the edge of the bar and nod at the bartender who dips his chin in acknowledgement.

The one bad thing about moving? Having to find a new bartender I love. The ones at this club treat me so well. It's a shame liquor isn't a good enough reason to keep me here.

"Well, have fun." Bella hops off her barstool and smacks a kiss on my cheeks. "He's super hot, by the way, even for a human."

I chuckle and bite my lip, peeking over at the man in question. He straightens when my sister skips away, standing over six-feet with broad shoulders. His navy shirt is tight enough to highlight how his middle tapers, and his dark washed jeans curl around thick thighs which are without a doubt all muscle.

This guy is as solid as a rock.

Yes, please.

I twinkle my fingers in his direction, and he smirks, the cocky smile making my stomach tighten with need.

"Is this spot taken?" His voice is a little nasally but that doesn't matter.

Soon enough, we won't be talking.

Maybe the universe doesn't hate me after all.

"Nope." I turn in his direction, crossing my legs and causing my black pencil skirt to ride up.

Shameless? Maybe.

Do I give a damn?

No.

The bartender, who I've decided is a literal godsend because he understands me without me having to say a word, slides me another martini. Seeing he added an extra olive, I grin at him in thanks. He winks, slides his gaze to my stranger, and shakes his head before walking off.

He knows the score, never gives me shit, and keeps the alcohol flowing. He's objectively my favorite being on this planet.

"What's your name?" He leans a little closer, his thigh brushing against my calf. Dropping his hand to his side, his fingers scarcely touch the skin above my knee.

The simple touch sends a zing of awareness through me.

Something about a man asking for what he wants with touches instead of words really appeals to me. *I want to fuck you* is all well and good, but an intentional brush of skin like this sends tingles down my spine. Unabashed desire, dilating pupils, and searing me with simple touches? Yeah. *That* is hot as hell.

"Bellatrix." I lift the pick and drag an olive off with my teeth, almost bursting into laughter when the guy sucks in a breath.

Way out of his depth, I see.

"Jason."

"Hm." I grab the next olive and lick my lips when I'm done chewing, feeling a sadistic amount of satisfaction when his gaze stays stuck on where my tongue moistened my mouth.

Sucker.

"Do you want to—"

"Moons, I thought you'd never ask." I toss the martini back like it's a shot, fight off a cough because, fuck, that's a lot of alcohol, and snatch his hand. "Follow me."

Jason doesn't respond or ask where we're going. His fingers clamp down around mine like he's afraid he'll lose me if he doesn't hold on, which isn't entirely wrong. He is going to lose me, but not before we have mind-blowing sex. Perhaps I'm being a bit reckless but thanks to my birth control implant and supernatural healing, I don't have to worry about pregnancy or STDs. All the more fun for me.

Jason and I walk to the back of the club, trying to find somewhere private. Scanning over my options, I debate on the usual spot in the supply closet or a riskier option that I've always wanted to try. I eye the stairs then glance over at the bar. The bartender is slammed—a line of women in a bridal party wait for their drinks. No barback in sight, probably off getting ice.

Perfect.

He'll be busy enough.

I let my gaze travel the room, quickly noting the discrete bouncers positioned throughout. As usual, they're too busy leering at the scantily clad females to pay attention to much else. It takes a full-on brawl to get their attention, so we're good to go.

Jason presses into my back, and his hand snakes around my waist, pulling me against his body as he gyrates his hips. I fight off a smile and shake my head at him.

"This way!" I shout over the music.

Taking the black stairs that run up the back wall of the club, I half jog up them in my heels, giggling when Jason starts whispering that this is a horrible idea or that we're going to get caught. We reach the top, and I spin and drop to my knees.

Jason's pupils blow wide, and I reach up into my hair, slipping out two bobby pins and winking at him. His face wrinkles for a second until I turn toward the door and slide the straight ends into the lock and begin working my magic.

"Oh my god," he murmurs. "You're horrible."

"I know," I sing-song.

A slight click and a twist and we're home free. Well, office free, but it's semantics at this point. Jason practically hauls me through the door and slams it closed. I chuckle and grab his neck, claiming his lips with mine. He growls when I nip his bottom lip and his hands find the back of my thighs. Being lifted off the ground by any man—human or supernatural—is hot as hell.

The office has a dim, overhead light, and it smells like stale cigarettes, but none of that is enough to kill the mood. My heart is racing, wondering how long we have until someone comes to throw us out of the club. Will they threaten to call the cops?

I can escape if they do, but the mere prospect of being handcuffed for this makes my pussy clench in need. Jason sets my ass on a desk and brushes aside some random crap so we have room. He's tall, but at this height, I can press against his erection to get some friction.

He yanks my silk top out of the skirt and over my head, taking in my full B cup. They're not huge, but I haven't had any complaints. I reach to undo my bra, helping speed up the process. Taking a moment, he steps away and undresses as fast as his human limbs will let him. When his hand fists around a rather impressive cock, I bite my cheek to keep from moaning.

Moons, I love the universe for this. I take back everything I ever said about her being a bitch.

My skirt is stretchy enough to hike up over my hips, so instead of taking it off like a normal, office-intruder person might, I shove it up and spread my legs. Jason makes a choked sound when he sees I'm not wearing any underwear.

Yeah, I came prepared for this.

I quirk my finger at him and lean back on my hands, taking all of him in as he struts over with all the swagger of a king. And to be honest, he kind of deserves to be cocky. This man obviously lives at the gym and drinks plenty of milk, because there isn't an inch of him that's squishy. His eyes rove over my body, catching on my pussy.

"Fuck."

I grin. "You like what you see?"

"Who are you?" he asks more to himself than me, stepping between my thighs and running his palms over them.

"Your friendly neighborhood vixen."

He laughs. I grab his dick, almost cackling when his laughter turns into a throaty moan. His velvety length fits perfectly against my center. I hold his head against my slick slit, sliding it up and down to wet it.

"Damn, girl."

His praise is very welcome, and I look up at him through my eyelashes, slowly curling my lips.

"What's my name?"

Furrowing his brow, he says, "Bellatrix."

"You're goddamn right." I line him up and grab both of his ass cheeks, yanking him against my body and forcing him inside of me, enjoying the way he slides in with ease. I'm so wet from the thrill of breaking in and fucking him in a stranger's office that there's zero resistance on my part.

I'm pretty sure his brain short-circuits because he tries to say something, but the words he forms are an incoherent string of curses and moans.

Exactly how I like them.

Catching up to the game, he grabs my sides and begins driving into me. His mouth crashes into mine in a sloppy, hungry kiss. His growls make my wolf perk up, but when she realizes he's only a human, she settles down.

She still hasn't gotten the *single for life* memo.

A faint buzzing sounds, so soft I almost miss it with Jason's noises and the music outside the room. Then it stops. I swipe my tongue against Jason's, reveling in the way he falls apart from being inside of me. Enjoying the way his cock throbs in direct response to my walls clamping around him.

Then the buzz comes again.

I break away from the kiss, and Jason's mouth seizes my neck, kissing and biting while he hammers into me. Turning my head to the side to give him better access, my eyes widen when they see a man who has to be in his late sixties standing near a filing cabinet tucked into the far corner of the room. He's balding, has a bit of a beer gut, and is wearing a skeezy bowling shirt with dark pants.

Jason doesn't notice, and I'll be damned if I stop him now because his thumb finds my clit. With a mischievous smile, I push my tits out, and the manager—because that has to be who this guy is—predictably drops his gaze.

Leaving him to his own devices, I focus on Jason. His lips

capture mine again, and his thrusts grow more violent and needy, but his thumb stays sure and focused on my sensitive bundle of nerves. My thighs quiver around his hips, and I gasp, relaxing my body to fully accept the orgasm that's about to crash over me.

It isn't long until we're both gasping and shouting our release, Jason's cum spilling into me and my hips bucking against his finger's ministrations. A sheen of sweat covers his body, and he blows out a hard breath, half-laughing half-groaning, and dropping his head against my shoulder.

"Can I keep you?"

"You can keep the memory," I say and pat his back. This is the part where he loses me. "But we should probably go because I think we're about to be in trouble."

"What?" he asks, lifting his head and searching my face.

I tip my head in the direction of our audience, who is now scarlet with his own need and a bit of irritation. Jason follows my gesture and curses, pulling away from me so fast I hiss at the sudden loss.

"Shit, man. Sorry."

Tossing my head back, I release a throaty chuckle.

What a way to leave this city.

two

BELLATRIX

My sister is in the middle of belting out her favorite line to a Riot Heart song, aiming and missing for the high note the lead singer hits, when my parents begin to slow down and turn on their blinker. I give her a look to say *nice try* and take the right turn onto a narrow, paved road lined by trees. I like to sing too, and she always tells me I should do it more, but I get nervous with her listening.

Fucking a stranger in a dirty office with an audience? No problem.

Singing in front of my family? Hell no.

Pack Ozark, the new pack my parents transferred to, is supposed to be better than the last one we were in. I don't have high hopes, especially since my dad is an omega. Other wolves basically take his lack of dominance as a free pass to abuse and torture him. My mom is a delta, so she's not much help when people start attacking him.

My sister and I are betas, but my sister doesn't like fighting much. I, on the other hand, don't mind a down and dirty brawl, especially when some asshole tries to kill my dad while he's on his morning walk. Hence our relocation. The last alpha didn't take kindly to me maiming his bitch-ass wolf. It was either move or eventually die, so we moved.

My Jeep's engine is a soft purr as we travel between the trees at a snail's pace. I tap my fingers to the beat of the song and shake my head at how slow they're driving.

"You know how Mom likes to look at everything," Bella says, the picture of patience.

"Yeah." I sigh and settle in. The road extends far into the trees, taking us deep into the woods.

Typical of most wolf packs, Pack Ozark tucks itself away far enough from humanity they don't have to worry about the dangers of living near humans. The closer we are to cities, the more the risk of exposure grows. Humans don't know about us, and per High Pack orders, it should remain that way. Besides, no one wants a war of races. The humans may be weaker, but their weapons are insane.

The more we drive, the more my mind wanders and recalls random stories I've heard lately.

"Did I tell you about what Zane told me?" I shoot my sister a quick glance.

"No." Bella pulls down the visor and checks over her hair and makeup. She's really worried about her first impression.

I catch my reflection in the rearview mirror and grimace. I washed my face, but the eyeliner from last night lingers around the edges of my eyelids and my hair is in a messy bun. My shirt reads *Fuck Off, I'm Reading* and my ripped shorts and chucks scream *I'm not here to impress you.*

Grinning at myself, I move my gaze to the road and Dad's taillights. They're still driving ridiculously slow, but I force myself to be patient. This is for their benefit, not mine. Dad needs a fresh start. He needs security and safety.

"I guess some wolf almost exposed herself to humans. She literally ran through a crowded college town in her other form," I say, resting my head back.

"Shut up." Bella pauses mid-lip gloss and raises her eyebrows. "What happened?"

Shrugging, I continue, "Zane said she ended up being sent to an island after her mate rejected her."

She sucks in a hard breath and caps her gloss. "Well, if she was rejected and feral, she needed to go."

"I didn't say she was feral." I frown at how defensive I sound. What do I care?

"She almost exposed herself to humans... sounds pretty feral to me."

Sucking in the side of my cheek, I say, "Rumor is she was attacked by a vampire or something."

"And you believe the rumor? What did her alpha do?"

"Sent her to the islands." I blow out a hard breath. "I don't know, okay. Zane just told me about it."

There are a dozen islands near upstate New York saved for rejected mates. The High Pack uses them as a prison for those who were turned away by their fated mates. The thing is, sometimes rejected mates go feral, and sometimes they don't. I hate the idea of the islands, because why keep shifters there who aren't feral? The whole concept seems cruel to me.

"Hm. Well, if he thought she needed to be sent there, we have to trust he did the right thing."

I don't tell her that sometimes alphas can be dicks because she hates when I talk like that. She doesn't like when I rip her rose colored glasses off and smash them into the concrete. So I let her live in oblivion and worry my lip as I think about the shifter who may or may not have been attacked by a vampire.

If she was attacked by a vampire, we should all be worried because the last time an attack like that happened was a long time ago. Things have been relatively calm between the wolves and vampires, but all it takes is one brutal murder to change that.

"Holy shit," I whisper when the giant house comes into view.

House isn't the right word. The pack house is a log cabin mansion. Light wood, elegant railings, and at least three stories high. I knew Pack Ozark was well off, but I didn't realize how well off. The wood is bright, probably freshly sealed for the weather, and the roof is a pretty dark color that offsets the lighter walls.

"Wow." Bella whistles and leans forward, craning her neck to see the roof. "Do you think they'll be safe here?"

I glance at her, noting the lines of concern wrinkling her eyes. "Anything is better than the last pack. Dad may be an omega, but he's an expert at adapting. Besides, a good alpha will realize his worth."

While he's not a great fighter, Dad knows a lot about engineering and can build just about anything. He's an asset.

Sitting back, she fidgets with the seat belt covering her chest. "I don't think I can watch him get hurt for much longer."

With a grimace, I throw the Jeep into park right behind where Dad parked and turn in my seat.

"I get it, more than you know, but we have to be careful now," I say in a hushed tone.

The radio is still playing, but if I were to talk any louder, there's no telling who might hear what we have to say, and I doubt the new alpha would take kindly to what my sister is implying.

"We're here now. Dad knows what to do to stay safe. The rest is out of our hands. We can always move again."

Her responding frown draws out my own.

"I hate moving."

I nod. "So do I, but it's not about us." With those words, I slip my keys out of the ignition, cutting the music off and opening my door.

My feet land on the soft grass next to the driveway, and I close the door with one hand, not bothering to turn around. I'm too busy gaping at our new home. Trees rise up like a tapestry behind the log cabin, completing the woodsy vibe.

Whoever built this place cleared the land immediately surrounding the home, because there's a small playground for kids, a net for volleyball, a few grills, picnic tables, and a large covered parking area for pack members.

All signs point to good things. So long as everyone in the pack is kind, we could live here for the rest of our lives. Mom releases a soft sigh and rests her head on Dad's shoulder. He loops his arm around her waist and there's a moment of complete peace.

Then it shatters so completely I wonder if I imagined it all along.

The double doors crash open, dozens of feet stampede out of the house and race toward the playground. Screams of excitement flutter in the air, carrying the powerful and unadulterated joy you can only find in a child's heart. A man walks out after them, a smirk tugging at his lips as he watches them run. His hair is a deep chestnut and side-swept, long enough to toe the line of maybe being man-bun worthy, but not quite that long. There is a bit of stubble covering his chin, like he forgot to shave this morning, and he's at least six-feet tall. His power signature reads as an alpha, but he doesn't have the enigmatic pull of a pack alpha.

Interesting. He must get along with the pack alpha because it isn't typical for more than one to live within the same pack.

Bella chuckles and bumps my hip with hers. "Wow, the teachers here are hot."

Her voice is low, but by design not quiet enough to escape his notice. The man standing at the top of the stairs snaps his gaze in our direction. Twin flames of amber lick over my sister before scorching me with their heat. Something in me threatens to break, like a board suspended between two pillars, stacked with weight upon weight until small fissures work through the wood, weakening it.

Another weight drops when his gaze clashes with mine, and I *snap*.

The weights crash to the ground, and every ounce of oxygen is dragged from my body with such force my shoulders curl forward.

His nostrils flare, and he takes two powerful steps down the stairs, not taking his eyes off of me for a second. Some invisible force begs me to race to him and jump into his arms, like this is some dramatic romance movie. I bite the inside of my lip and plant my feet, fighting the pull.

My wolf whimpers in my head, whispering things to me with her pitiful animal noises I can't acknowledge. Things about love and eternity and destiny.

No. I won't acknowledge what she's trying to tell me because it's insanity.

Bella gasps and grabs my arm when he growls low in his chest before prowling toward me like he wants to simultaneously rip my head off and kiss me stupid.

Cue stomach flop. My vision tunnels until all I can see are those irises. He stops a few feet away from me, and fresh pine wraps around me. Inviting and familiar. Tremors work through my body, and my wolf bays for this man inside of my head. She can't speak with words, but it doesn't take a genius to figure out what she wants. My wolf has been a steady presence in my mind, but the only time she really makes herself known is when I'm threatened. Only, I don't feel that way now.

I feel something I shouldn't feel at all according to statistics. An emotion and longing I've long since written off stirs inside of me.

"Mate."

"Don't," I say when he steps forward and reaches for me.

His hand pauses in the air before he decides to ignore my request. He wraps his fingers around my hip and guides me toward him. Like a mind numb idiot, I allow him to manhandle me. I allow him to look down at me. I allow him to slowly lower his face to mine, letting him take a good look before I allow him to bury his nose in the crook of my neck.

He moans, and his stubble scrapes against my skin. I stand completely still, hands at my sides and fingers clenched into fists so tight my knuckles have turned white. Even though it makes zero sense, I'm desperate to touch him, but I know the thing driving me doesn't give a damn about what's logical because he's my destiny.

No. No flipping way.

There's no way this man is my fated, but the way my wolf howls in triumph tells me he is exactly that.

His grip turns bruising the longer his nose stays stuck against my skin, and a savage growl works its way out of his body. My heart skips a beat, and my wolf cowers, wondering what we've done to make him angry. The bond between fated mates is unmatched by any other type of relationship, so I'm not surprised to find I know he's mad and that some-how, I'm the one who made him that way.

"You smell like a human."

I gulp, hating the gravel and disgust coloring his tone.

Sexual relations with humans are generally frowned upon, but I know that's not why he's mad. Oh no. He's mad because I'm not pure. Our society covets virginity, especially when it comes to finding your fated mate. The person the moon molded to fit you only deserves your most pure self. Since most fated mates find each other at a younger age, a lot of wolves don't end up having sex and finding someone else to take as a mate—a nonmoon-blessed joining, but some-thing that can be born out of love and respect.

That sort of bond never interested me. I wanted fate or I wanted nothing, and here fate is seconds away from savaging my throat if the way his teeth brush against my neck are any indication. There's no explaining the way my stomach quivers or the way my eyes widen with panic.

He can't be mad at me. I don't want him to be. Stupid bond; it's messing with me already. We've only been in each other's presence for a few minutes and I want nothing more than to make him happy. To earn his approval.

My stomach churns, threatening to heave under his unwarranted anger. That reaction alone tells me perhaps my wolf is right. He *is* my fated.

He is my forever and he is my destiny.

My eyebrows pinch as I turn over the idea of being with someone so alive with rage. Is that really the future I want for myself?

His snarl intensifies when I don't respond. "Why?"

Listen, I've never hidden who I was from the world, and I'm not about to start now. Fated mate be damned, I won't lose myself to appease him. He growls again, grip tightening.

I swallow and say, "I was with someone last night."

Wrong answer. The pads of his fingers hurt, but I press my lips together to hold back what I want to say because his body vibrates with anger. When his teeth actually clamp down on my skin, dull pain tugs at my muscles.

There goes my fantasy of a prince swooping in to save me and carry me off in a happily ever after ending. This is nothing like my childhood vision.

"You're hurting me." I calmly place my hands on his chest and shove.

He doesn't budge, nor does he release his hold on me. Those teeth bite down harder. Sometimes the initial seizing of the bond can be primal, making a person forget their humanity and give in to their wolfish side. He wants to punish me for having sex, he's pissed, and he doesn't listen.

Even though it'll make my wolf mad, I slam my knee between his legs, hitting him right in his jewels and shoving him back at the same time. His teeth drag across my skin before he stumbles back, clutching his junk and spearing me with a look of pure hatred.

"You're not a virgin."

Ah, the archaic desires of males and their pricks destroying my chance of happiness.

Moon forbid I enjoy myself.

I scoff and put my hand on my hip. "I'm twenty-seven. A bit old for a chastity belt, don't you think?"

"Bellatrix!" My mother's voice rises three octaves, shrill and terrified.

Wincing, I cast a glance at my parents. Bella's wide eyes find mine over my dad's shoulder. She must have run to them when she realized whatever was happening wasn't good. Can't say I blame her. Remembering we're here for Dad and his safety, I soften my features and drop my gaze.

"I'm sorry, Mate." Yeah. Nope. My words sound pissed off through clenched teeth. So much for being soft.

"You're not my mate." He surges forward, grabbing my arms and dragging me closer. "My mate would never whore herself out with a human."

So, maybe there is another thing you need to know. I despise the word whore. I hate the word slut. I especially hate that a woman taking charge of her sex life and living as so many men do automatically places her in either of those categories. So when he says the word *whore*, my blood boils so hot it's a miracle my body doesn't combust where I stand.

Almost on instinct, I hock the biggest wad of saliva from the back of my throat and spit it in his rude ass face. The glob lands on his nose, but part of it hits his eye, and he pinches it shut, hissing out a sharp breath I can feel stabbing through me like he took a literal knife and gutted me.

Five minutes in and I already hate this fated bond. It's not complete, not by a long shot, but by finding him and being near him, the beginnings of a life-altering connection have started to forge. Which is why I know he wants to punch me. If I didn't see it in the way his lips curl back, I'd have felt it in the way his entire being goes preternaturally still. A predator preparing to eviscerate its prey. Gleaming, beady black eyes of a snake as it rears its head back, hissing and spitting venom before launching for the kill strike.

"Chad."

Somehow the new voice pulls him out of his head, and he snaps his eyes open and glares over his shoulder at a man who looks exactly like him, only a bit older. A brother, maybe? Too young to be his father.

"She's my fated," Chad—side note: why the hell is my fated named Chad? Not fucking cool—snaps at the newcomer.

"Then why are you hurting her?" The man, who may as well be my rescuer at this point, hops off the porch and rushes toward us. "You need to let her go." The soft command rolls over me. This is the alpha, but Chad is either strong enough to ignore his words or the bond is giving him the ability to ignore it.

"She's not a virgin." Chad's words slice through the air, and his brother stumbles to a stop.

His gaze scans my body in a clinical way, and then he sniffs, repulsion lifting the side of his top lip as his eyes flash with an echo of his brother's disgust. Recovering from his surprise, he walks toward us with purpose coloring his face bright red.

Clearing his throat, he grabs Chad's wrist. "Let her go."

"No, Garry," Chad says.

Dropping my head back and letting out an exaggerated sigh, I ask the moon what I did to deserve this.

The weight of their stares burn into me, but I continue to look at the sky. There are a few clouds, but no sign of any magical fairy coming down to save me from whatever is happening.

"You know what you have to do." Garry's pointed and whispered words bring me back to reality with a hard slap.

Oh, hell no.

He wouldn't dare.

I struggle to get out of Chad's hold, but he squeezes me tighter, searing me with his scorching gaze which has turned from alluring to spiteful. Something shifts between us, and I know he's preparing to break whatever has started, to ruin me for good and leave me broken.

A shell of the woman I used to be.

Rejected mates are pitiful beings, forlorn and pathetic. Sometimes they go crazy. Sometimes they grow feral. Which is why what he's about to do has my breath quickening. Rejected mates get shunned to the islands, carted away to be kept like prisoners because the elders think we'll be the reason shifters are exposed to the world.

No.

He can't win. He can't break me.

He can't.

He can't.

"I—"

"I reject you," I say in a rush, beating him to the punch. "I don't want you or your wolf. Now. Let. Me. Go." When I shove away this time, he lets me go.

The growl he unleashes makes the frantic pitter-patter of my heart thud, growing heavier with every beat. Every instinct is telling me I'm right, but the stupid bond has me feeling a mess of emotions. My chest aches with how I've hurt him. My wolf wants to shift so she can rub against him to beg him for forgiveness, marking him with her scent. My eyes water when the words settle and rip through me like claws, taking what little is left of my heart and obliterating it in a harsh swipe.

I take a hard breath, clutching my chest. The bond had barely started. What would it feel like if it were fully settled? Thank god I don't have to find out.

"Trix?" Bella whines.

My parents stay silent. I'm not mad at them because this is my trouble. Dad just got here, and I won't taint him any more than I already have by calling for them to help.

I've already royally screwed this up. I seal my mouth shut and place a protective barrier over my heart in the form of my now bruised arms locking together.

Chad takes a step forward, snarling at me. "You can't reject me, because I reject you."

The words crash into me like a freight train, derailing my own sense of triumph as the two rejections war with one another. I've never seen a confrontation like this between fated mates, but I suspect, as with anything in the shifter world, the stronger the wolf, the more likely they are to prevail.

The beta in me is ready for a fight, but his alpha strength courses through me like a taser, lighting up my nerves with punishing pain and ensuring I'll remember one thing. His words are stronger. His rejection is stronger. He wins.

He rejected me.

three

BELLATRIX

"If you're done with your dramatics, follow me." Garry turns, and though he hasn't claimed me as one of his wolves, the alpha's words strike a chord within me.

No matter what I'm feeling or how much I hurt, I can't resist his pull. Cursed power dynamics. If only I were an alpha, then I could resist him.

My feet move of their own accord, and I glance back at Bella, seeing the tracks of ruined mascara covering her cheeks. Mom is clutching Dad's shirt like it's the only thing between her and falling to the ground. I meet worried, loving eyes and gently shake my head. There's nothing my father can do now. My fate is sealed, and it's not with a mate.

I'm a reject.

Moon be damned, I'm rejected.

Because I'm not a virgin.

This is absolute bullshit. I'm sure Chad isn't a virgin either, but like with almost every society I've ever heard of, it's not the man's chastity that matters. Only the women get the shit end of the stick. Only we have to be demure virgins, pure and untouched to make their egos flare.

Like I said, complete bullshit.

Trudging up the steps, fighting off the pain of the bond breaking, I pant. Garry scowls at me over his shoulder like I've personally offended him by breathing too loud, so I let out another heavy breath.

He snaps the door open, and I barely catch it before it slams shut, shoving through like a moody teenage girl on her first period. Garry paces in the big sitting room, casting furtive glances my way. I step farther into the space, noticing he subtly moves back, putting more distance between us like he believes what I have will catch and soon enough he'll be ruined too.

Clenching my fingers into fists, I stare at him until he stops pacing. He turns his gaze on me, not the weighted stare of an alpha unleashing his power, but the deadly watchfulness of a predator.

"As you know, I have no choice in the matter."

I dig my nails into my palm, ignoring the painful cramp in my stomach. "You don't have to do it. I'm not pack. You never claimed me. Let me go."

"I can't allow that to happen." He shakes his head. "It's too dangerous. The elders issued an official order. You know what that means."

Biting my tongue, I keep my mouth sealed shut even though I could recite the order verbatim.

High Pack Notice: All rejects must report to Wolfe Island for immediate processing and island assignment.

Rejected Mates weren't always sequestered to the middle of nowhere. A few feral rejects ruined any chance of a normal life for the others. Now, out of misplaced fear and panic, the elders—also known as the High Pack—like to send the ones who were rejected away. Send us away. Chad gets to stay since his rejection trumped mine. He's now the rejector, and the rules don't apply to the rejectors, only the rejected.

Everything I planned for myself, from vacations, simple holidays with the family, and maybe even adoption fly out the window. A loose paper snatched by a harsh gust of wind and plunged into the brutal reality of the outside world.

Trampled on.

Driven over.

Rain drenched.

I'm not sure what future me will look like now and that terrifies me. I pride myself on being brave and spontaneous, on not being easily intimidated. Uncertainty shouldn't make me so nervous, but it does, and I hate it.

Garry starts talking, but I don't catch what he says because my chest tightens. Pressure builds, crushing my lungs until I can't breathe. The room closes in on me, the soft flow of air from the vents stings my skin, and my legs begin to shake. Thousands of invisible needles prick me.

My life is essentially over.

Because of Chad.

I'll kill him.

The violent thought tears me out of my panic, and I make my way toward the door on quick feet, swinging my fist at Garry's face when he catches me around the waist.

"STOP."

My body slackens at his command, and I try again to raise a fist, but my limbs don't respond. The power of an alpha bearing down on a beta is too much. He has me paralyzed; my mind is screaming at me to do something, anything to get away from this place. I have to escape.

"We don't have to do this the hard way." He searches my face, and I feel the left side of my lip curl in response. "But you're not going to stop fighting, are you?"

Pursing my lips, I refuse to answer him.

"I'm going to have to restrain you then."

"Don't hurt my family."

He rears his head back like I smacked him. "What kind of alpha do you think I am?"

A beast. A terrible wolf. An asshole. A tiny little prick in desperate need of a good lay.

"I don't know what you're thinking, but your eyes give

you away. You can hate me all you want, but it won't change my decision. You're going to Wolfe Island for processing. What happens to you after that is their decision."

"Fuck you." I thrash in his arms, attempting to break free of his iron hold, but it's no use. Not only does he have supernatural strength, he's much stronger than I am because he's an alpha.

I still try though, aiming a kick between his legs. Catching my foot with his knee, he knocks my strike off course and growls. Something hits the back of my head hard enough I yelp, blinking back the black spots suddenly spilling across my vision.

"Did you have to hit her?" Chad asks as the room dims. When did he get here?

It's only morning, so I'm not sure why it's gotten so dark.

"She'll be easier to handle this way." Garry's words are the last thing I hear.

SOMETIME LATER, I WAKE UP STRAPPED TO A CHAIR. THIN silver chains crisscross over my forearms and around my ankles. I scream when the hurt registers, knowing the longer the chains are on, the more painful it'll be. The silver won't kill me unless it gets into my bloodstream, but touching it hurts like a bitch. My throat is raw, making me wonder if I've woken up yelling once before.

I rock back and forth, trying to tip the chair over. It won't budge. Almost like they've bolted it to the ground. That or I'm too weak to move at all. For all my attempts to free myself, I'm rewarded with nothing but agony. I whimper, despising how weak I sound.

Thunderous steps pound down the hallway, heading toward the room I'm in. The simple bedroom is warm and welcoming if you don't count me being held prisoner as part of the woodsy aesthetic.

Swinging wide, the door opens, and Chad steps through. I scream again, cursing him for this and begging to be set free all in the same rant. His gaze flits over me, and a tiny trickle of regret fills his annoyingly beautiful irises. The look gives me pause, and I stop all of my thrashing and yelling. He wants to see me rabid, to see me break because of his rejection.

This fucker came in here for some sort of validation, to know he did the right thing.

Staring him down, I grind my jaw.

"You know this had to be done."

"Screw you." I spit at his feet.

The muscle in his neck jumps when he clenches his teeth. "I came in here to see if maybe we could talk through our differences, but I guess I was wrong."

"Our differences? You rejected me because I'm not a virgin! This isn't the fucking middle ages, *Chad*."

"Don't talk to me like that." His voice cracks through the air, and I recoil in my seat, hating the fact that he affects me at all. "Good, much better. If you could keep that mouth shut, I would have considered taking you back."

My body flushes with rage. Thank the moon I'm rejected because being mated to him would have been the worst experience of my life. I guess fate can find you a partner, but it can't fix shitty attitudes.

Narrowing my eyes, I clamp my mouth shut and wait him out. Seeing as he told me he wanted me to shut up, I don't understand why annoyance flashes across his face. Then it clicks. He wants me to be strong. Even though he doesn't want this, his wolf wants a mate that's dominant and won't be pushed around, just like my wolf doesn't want him to be mad at me.

I make the decision to look at the floor and refuse to meet his gaze. The more I pretend to be weak and unworthy, the more his wolf will be disgusted by me. A few minutes later he scoffs, spinning on his heel and storming out of the door with heavy footsteps.

Pinching my eyes shut, I take a shaky breath, realizing how tired I am. My mind has been racing, trying to figure out if there's a way to escape my fate, but I'm starting to understand there isn't a way out of this.

Whether I like it or not, I'm getting sent to an island.

four

BELLATRIX

The transport team arrives a few hours later. I can't even find it in me to muster up a fight. They take the chains off, which draws a strangled gasp from me, but otherwise I don't react to the burns coating my skin. My entire body aches from the bond breaking, and I can't differentiate between the pain of the wounds and the hurt of the rejection.

I can't imagine what it would feel like if the bond had fully taken hold.

Not bothering to look at the two men, I stare at a spot on the wall as they yank me from the chair. They grip me so tight I wonder if they expected more of a fight. I walk, keeping up with their unhurried pace with ease and don't bother giving them hell. The silver must have drained my energy more than I thought, because there's no way I'd go this willingly if I were at full strength.

My sister squeaks from down the hall and races to me. The guards shout at her to stop, but she ignores them and launches herself at me, latching on to me like a monkey. Her embrace is suffocating, and ultimately the sound of her crying gets to me. The dam breaks and tears pour out of me hard and fast. Bella's body shakes, and she sniffs, wiping her nose with the back of her hand.

"Please, don't take her," she begs the men, but their hold tightens on me once more. Not even her pretty face and broken heart will sway them.

"Bella," Dad says, placing his hand on her back.

Our gazes meet and hold. His shine with moisture, and guilt gnaws at me for breaking down so hard. The more I show my pain, the more it will hurt them. A steady breath is all I need to tuck away the shuddering pants. There's nothing I can do for my wet cheeks but to stop crying.

"Trixie," he whispers in such a tender voice I almost start weeping again.

"It's okay." I glance away, not able to look him in the eye when I speak such a blatant lie.

Bella fights him when he begins to pry her off, but when he scolds her, she deflates and climbs off of me.

"I'll miss you so much."

I gasp, but manage to keep a hold of my emotions. "B-squared for life," I murmur, reminding her of what we used to refer to ourselves as when we were little.

Her lip trembles, and the guys holding me seem to run out of patience because they shoulder past my dad and sister, dragging me through the cabin with their quick steps. Mom is waiting by the door, a hard frown marring her pretty face. She doesn't say anything, but she doesn't have to. There's nothing but love in her soft green eyes, and I can hear everything she can't seem to say out loud.

She loves me.

Be safe.

She wishes this weren't happening.

You'll be okay, Trix.

Dipping my chin, I acknowledge her silent thoughts. "I love you, Mom."

A single, fat tear traces down her porcelain skin. Realizing I've caused my family enough pain, I start to walk as fast as the men, passing through the door, across the yard, and getting inside their SUV without protest. Silver handcuffs are snapped in place around my wrists, but not even the instant spark of pain bothers me. If anything, it helps take my mind off of what's happening.

Resting my head against the cool window pane, I watch the landscape pass by, soaking up every mile and memorizing it. Maybe if I can call my family, I'll be able to understand the places they refer to.

I don't even know if they allow phones. My pockets are empty. I don't have my purse. They didn't grab my suitcase, so all I have that's mine are the clothes I'm wearing.

"How long will the drive take?"

"Don't speak."

"Fuck you," I mutter to the gruff guy, which only makes him chuckle.

Neither of the men talk to me the rest of the way. I knew rejects were looked down on, but I didn't realize how shitty they were treated. Eventually, we make it to a private airport with one small strip for landing and taking off. The sleek black vehicle comes to a hard stop fifty yards away from a plane.

The cuffs stay on as one of the guys unbuckles and helps me out of the SUV. I hold my chin high, walking up the stairs and into the plane like I'm not being carted off to Hell. I'm roughly put in a seat, and the men sit in the spots directly across from me. This plane isn't like a commercial one, there are only a dozen seats, and the rows face each other, like whoever bought this plane planned on having lengthy conversations with their travel companions.

"I expected some screaming." The one who not so nicely told me not to speak gives me a smirk.

Looking at him, I merely lift an eyebrow and shrug. "It won't change anything." I yawn and a wave of exhaustion crashes into me. I fight to keep my eyes open as the air in the cabin switches on. We're about to take off.

"The silver is making you tired. You should sleep. We'll be

there in a few hours." This comes from the other guy. There's no pity in his eyes, only cold observation.

No sympathy for the broken, I guess.

Given my options of staring at them the entire ride, avoiding their gazes, or sleeping, I choose a nap.

The rest I do get isn't enough, and I'm not able to relax to truly let my guard down and slip into dreamland. The flight attendant, who must get paid extremely well, comes to give them drinks, but she completely ignores me. Since I'm pretending to sleep, I can't tell if it's because I look like I don't want to be disturbed or because they don't think I deserve the decency of being offered a refreshment.

Sometimes, ignorance is bliss.

When the pilot announces our arrival, I sit up and glance out of the window, catching sight of a body of water. I spot a bridge, which connects Wolfe Island to the mainland, and then we fly lower and lower until we land on another tiny runway. Trees surround the airport, and the rocky terrain reminds me of Colorado. We're somewhere north of upstate New York though, not in the middle of the country.

"Time for processing."

I'm yanked up by my biceps, and I growl at the men. "I can walk on my own."

"There's the spark," the gruff one says. "Sorry, doll. I've been fooled one too many times by a pretty face. If you try to run, it means I have to catch you. Then the elders find out, and no one wants that to happen. Trust me and be a good girl."

Glaring at him, I lean into his hold, wondering if I can get in a headbutt. "I'm not a good girl."

"Apparently not. Isn't that how you ended up in this situation?"

"Asshole," I seethe, but he shrugs and leads me to the front of the plane.

"Hey, I'm being honest. If you ask me, I don't mind a more experienced woman, if you know what I'm saying, but I'm not your fated." He walks in front of me as we go down the stairs, holding on to the handcuffs.

"Stop. Talking." The other guy, the one who must be in charge of this mission, breathes down my neck, forcing me to go faster.

I shudder when my feet hit the concrete and scoot to the side so he's not at my back.

"Don't talk to her."

"Whatever," the other guy, who I guess is now the nice guy instead of the gruff guy, mutters.

"You two are real peaches, you know that?"

They both scowl at me before ignoring me.

I guess that ends the conversation portion of *Let's Destroy Bellatrix's Life.*

PROCESSING WAS A STERILE AND UNNERVING EVENT. THE CASE worker who took care of me hardly looked at me, only asked me a few pointed questions, tsked, and pursed her lips. The most annoying thing of all was when she muttered *what a shame.* Being cuffed makes more sense now after that, because had I had free use of my hands, I might have bitch-slapped her.

The boat I'm riding in hits a wave, jolting me to the side. I reach up and grasp the oh-shit bar on the back of the seat in front of me. My two guards still won't talk to me, but I've deduced that there will be no driving to the island I've been assigned to.

Wolfsbane Island.

How fitting.

Dark blue water ripples, cresting in white tips as the sleek speedboat cuts through it. We pass a few islands before the captain takes a sharp left and heads toward a small dock. Through the generous smattering of trees, I can make out the shapes of a few large homes. There is no beach, only steel colored rocks lining the steep rim of the land. The ruddy brown dock is worn and in need of a fresh coat of sealant, but the captain doesn't seem to be the least bit worried about tying his boat to the rundown post.

My neck pricks with awareness and the hair there rises, warning me that someone is watching me. I glance at the guards, but they're talking to the captain, which means whoever it is, is on the island.

"All right, princess. Here's your new home."

I ignore the guard as he helps me off the boat and study the trees, trying to find the spy. Spy is probably an exaggeration, but this is a private moment and they have no right to watch me being dumped here. Though if I lived here, I'd probably be watching the arrivals as well.

We reach the end of the dock, and he unlocks the cuffs. I glance down and watch as they remove them from my wrists. My skin hasn't healed yet, if it even will, and the flesh where the cuffs rubbed is raw and angry.

"Good luck," the nice guard says with a hint of amusement. "You're going to need it."

I glance at him, taking in his proximity, the smirk on his face, and make a decision I'll probably come to regret. Curling my fingers into a fist, I punch him in the face, enjoying the immediate rush of blood as his nose breaks.

"Not again," the quiet one says.

Turning to give him the same reaction, I stop when I see a black baton pointed at my chest. He presses a button and it zaps, electricity jumps between the two metal prongs at the end.

"You shouldn't have done that." He moves faster than I can, and the prod jams into my stomach.

"Oh, fu—" My words are cut off when he turns the taser on and white clouds my vision. Every muscle in my body tenses, and I'm stuck convulsing where I stand as lightning courses through me. I hear a scream, not registering the sound is coming from me until he stops pressing the small black button and steps back. It takes another few seconds for me to stop yelling and for my body to relax. My knees give out, and he scoffs. I try to look at him, but I can't lift my head.

The world tilts. My body thuds to the ground, sharp rocks biting into my skin. The guards must leave because I hear the sputtering motor start before it speeds away, leaving me on the ground like roadkill.

"Fuck," I finally say, the word comes out muffled since my cheek is pressed into the ground.

What now?

five

CREED

She looks so small lying on the ground. I can't believe she punched the guard, but damn did it make me grin like a fool to see crimson coating the dick's face. The guy she hit was the same one who brought me to the island, so I know he deserved it. He was an asshole, taunting me about being a reject and telling me I wouldn't make it more than a few days.

Once I make sure she's breathing and not in immediate danger, I back away from the tree trunk I'm hiding behind, turning to head back to the house to tell the guys.

Wolfsbane's population went down by one this morning, but now it's back to ten. I guess the High Pack thought we needed a replacement for George. Other than flagging down the guard boat when one passed by, there has been no discussion on what happened. Like they don't even care that he was murdered. The guard who showed up was supposed to report it to the proper authorities for an investigation, but he was less than sympathetic when we showed him what happened.

The murder part is my own theory, which I have yet to prove, but I highly doubt George impaled himself on a giant metal rod.

He was killed by someone on this island.

Seeing as the woman is the only one who isn't a suspect, I feel a little bad for leaving her behind, but I've learned my lesson the hard way. You can't trust strangers, especially not rejects. She may seem mostly sane now, but she could already be going feral. Those wolves are dangerous and typically end up being put down.

For now, she'll have to fend for herself.

~

BELLATRIX

I wake up with a headache and a dry mouth. Note to self: never get tasered again. Tiny drops of rain pepper my skin, and I push off the ground, kneeling and glancing around. The boat is long gone. The dock is deserted, and there isn't a person in sight. Surely this island isn't deserted, right?

They've been sending rejects to the islands for a few years now, so I doubt this one is empty. Besides, I remember the sensation of being watched earlier. I know at least one other shifter lives on this island. Hopefully they're not crazy. It would be just my luck to be stranded on an island with a feral wolf.

Blowing out a hard breath to move my hair out of my eyes, I peer into the trees. They're not too thick, so I can see houses and narrow roads. This place looks fully developed, which is odd considering they're putting rejects here.

Did they evacuate the islands or were they abandoned?

The rain picks up, pelting me with big drops, and I scowl at the gray and black sky. What do they say? When it rains it pours? Yeah, that about sums it up. Shoving off the rock infested grass, I carefully pick my way through the trees. Nothing has been mowed in this thicker part, and I end up having to dodge more than a few poison ivy plants.

The closer I get to the road, which I can now see loops around a circular drive before shooting off and curving in another direction, the more I notice imperfections. Weeds cropping up across all the lawns, broken shutters, even a few shattered windows and chipped siding. I glance down the road, standing on the edge of the curb and waiting for a car to come screeching around the bend.

No engines, no squealing tires, and no sounds.

Lightning cracks above me, a jagged flash of yellow slicing across the sky.

There is no way they left me here on my own, right?

I step onto the road, scanning the houses. These all appear empty, and I'm getting soaked, so I pivot in the direction of the house on the left, a simple light blue cottage with a covered porch, and race toward it. The houses are two stories and surrounded by trees. They block my view so I can't tell what lies around the bend in the road, but now isn't the time to explore. Thudding up the steps, I cross the porch in two seconds and fling the screen door back, praying the front door isn't locked.

Luck is on my side for one thing it seems. The knob twists with ease and the door opens with a light squeak. I step inside the home, quickly shut the door, and rest my back against the stained glass. I bang my head against the window twice, releasing a hard breath before taking a second to glance around. For being abandoned, the house is clean. I glance at my shoes, wondering how muddy they are, then glance at the runner rug leading down the entryway and into an open concept living and kitchen area.

I ease away from the door, stepping on the tile instead of the rug as I make my way down the short hallway. There are still pictures on the wall from the previous owners, and in the frames are smiling faces with straight teeth, polo shirts, and khakis. A family of four used to live here, parents and two girls. I run my finger over the sisters, shoving the sharp ache in my chest down at the thought of Bella.

I can't think about it, or I'll get overwhelmed, so I move

on from the pictures and head to the living room. The decor isn't stuffy, but you can tell the couches cost at least three-thousand dollars apiece and the mahogany entertainment center stretches across half of one wall. A sixty-inch T.V. sits prominently in the middle, and trinkets or books line the shelves around it. The big bay window facing the street has the curtains open, but with the storm, it's dark in here. I scan the wall for a light switch, snapping it up when I find it.

The light on the ceiling fan flickers to life, much to my surprise, and I take a better look around. This place isn't clean, it's spotless. About the time my brain catches the warning flag is the time I hear the whoosh of a pan aimed at my head. I scream and drop to the ground, rolling away from the woman with crazed eyes.

"Get the hell out of my house!" she yells, swinging her arms back for another hit. Her movements are so savage her brown hair flies out behind her. Her wolf energy flares around her. She's a beta too, and winning a fight against her isn't guaranteed.

She could be stronger than me. I don't have enough energy to fight after the silver restraints and cuffs. I should have shifted earlier to heal myself, but I didn't, a stupid mistake to make on my part.

I scramble away from her, putting the couch between us and holding up my hands. "I'm sorry! I thought it was empty."

"Well it's not!" She narrows her eyes and flits her gaze over my body. "I don't recognize you. You must be new."

How observant of her. Really, gold stars all around.

"I'm Bellatrix." I glance around. "I'm sorry I came in without permission."

"Harlow," she says, tossing the pan on the couch. "Normally, I'd kick you out, but judging by the marks on your skin, you've already been treated like shit enough."

A hollow laugh works out of me. "You could say that." I lower my arms and shift on my feet, wincing when my shoes squelch.

Harlow sighs and shakes her head. "I just cleaned too. If you're staying, take your shoes off."

She doesn't have to tell me twice. I take them off, peeling the wet socks off as well, and carry them to the front door, keenly aware of her gaze tracking my every movement. She may have put the weapon down, but she hasn't relaxed. I set my shoes on the tile, and walk on the carpet to avoid the muddy footprints I left behind when I first came in. A quick glance at the photos confirms Harlow isn't in them. This wasn't her home to begin with. She must have claimed it.

When I return to the living room, we stare at each other for an awkward few seconds. Lightning flashes and a boom of thunder chases after it like they're playing tag.

Clearing my throat, I jerk my thumb over my shoulder, pointing to the mess. "I can clean that up."

Her eyes lower to the floor, and I swear I see the skin under her left one twitch. "It's fine. I'll do it."

"I don't mind. After all, I'm the one who made the mess."

"It's fine," she snaps, so I shut my mouth and try not to pull a face that'll end up with us at odds again.

I really don't want to be stuck in the rain.

"Wait here. No funny business." She glares at me before going to grab her supplies.

With nothing better to do, I watch the sheets of rain, wondering if the sky somehow absorbed the tears I've been holding back. Harlow returns, muttering under her breath about mud and the inconvenience I've caused her. I don't point out she's the one who decided she didn't want help, because that won't help anything.

She scrubs the floor so hard I'm surprised the mop

doesn't break, and when she finishes, she slams it into the mop bucket, casting her eyes in my direction.

"Come on. I have clothes that might fit you."

Chewing on my cheek, I follow after her, politely waiting while she puts away the cleaning supplies. I have a million questions for her but for now, I'll wait. She's already annoyed with me, and I doubt talking her ear off will help me get into her good graces. She's actually the first person aside from my family to be somewhat kind to me after being rejected. Everyone else has treated me like a disease.

She leads me down a hall next to the kitchen and into a bedroom. Beach decor lines the walls; a rope wrapped around a picture frame, a miniature helm, a shelf with a sailboat. Soft blue and gray paint, an azure comforter, and a white dresser.

"You're about a size eight?"

"Or a ten if I eat pizza," I quip.

This time when she looks at me, the edges of her mouth twist up. "The best we have around here is homemade."

"No restaurants then? How disappointing. I heard this place had great reviews."

She laughs, and I cheer myself on. Sarcasm works about seventy percent of the time, the other thirty percent, well, we won't talk about that. Harlow is pretty when she's not trying to murder me with a pan, and her soft green eyes light with mirth.

"You can never believe the reviews on Yelp." Opening a drawer of the dresser, she digs around for a second before pulling out a simple red tank-top and shorts. "This should fit. There's a brush and hair ties in the top drawer." She gestures to the dresser.

"Thank you."

Nodding, she tips her head to the side. "I was going to make tea. Do you want some?"

"Sure."

Flicking her brown hair over her shoulder, she gives me another once-over before she leaves.

I take my shirt and pants off, setting my wet clothes on the floor and spreading them out to dry since there isn't a bathroom. Her reaction to the mud I tracked in is enough to tell me she's a clean freak, and I know she wouldn't appreciate me dripping water everywhere by carrying the damp clothes with me to ask what I should do with them.

My bra is soaked, and while I hate to part with the only one I have with me, I toss it onto the pile before yanking on the top. The material immediately gets wet from my hair, but I'm drier than I was before. I keep my underwear on because they're only a little wet, so at least there's that.

I scoff, shaking my head as I slip into the shorts. One pair of underwear. I must be rich! My hair is a mess, so I use the brush to work out the knots. I make a ponytail and use an elastic around my hair. Grabbing a few bobby pins lying in a plastic dish and sticking them in the back, I pin up the errant strands. This is as good as it's going to get, so I head off to the kitchen, hoping this time Harlow won't try to hit me.

SIX

RONAN

Thunder rolls over the island about the time Creed bursts in the house and storms into the kitchen. Glancing over at him from my table in the dining room, I set the card down where I'd intended then lean back in my chair, pausing my game of solitaire.

"Why do you look pissed?" I ask, scanning his pinched face.

"I'm not." He grabs a towel from the kitchen counter and scrubs it over his short blond hair.

"Right," I drawl, tapping my fingers on the arms of the leather computer chair.

The room used to have a fancy twelve-seater table, but the guys and I decided it was a bit stuffy for our taste, so instead we pilfered some computer desks and killer ergonomic chairs from the other rooms. Whoever lived here before Wolfsbane became a home for rejects really cared about their lumbar support.

"We have a new person."

Ah. That sort of explains the scowl.

"And?" I hedge, waiting for him to tell me everything about his interaction with the person. Something tells me it didn't go well, either the newcomer is a jerk or a woman.

"She broke a guard's nose."

A woman, that explains it. Creed has been here the longest, around four years, and he's sexually frustrated to say the least. The only other woman on the island is Harlow, but she'd be more likely to castrate us before taking any of us to bed, so it's fair to say our grip strength has gotten really strong and our wrists can work overtime.

"What did the guard do?"

His lips twitch. "The other one tased her."

"Of course he did. Sounds like quite the afternoon. Was she nice?" I scoot my chair back and go to the kitchen to grab a beer from the fridge. We lucked out with alcohol because this house had two beer coolers in the garage packed full of the cheap stuff. We use it sparingly, when the occasion calls for it, and I'd say this is one of those times.

"Want one?"

Creed shakes his head, so I shrug and screw the cap off and take a swig. "Was she nice?" I ask again, raising an eyebrow when he twists his mouth to the side.

"I didn't stay to find out."

"Damn, man. That's cold." I scratch my short beard, watching him work through his own frustration. "Even I wouldn't do that and you always tell me I'm an asshole."

"That's because you *are* an asshole," he says, hopping onto the counter and sitting. "We don't know anything about her."

Glancing at the clock on the stove, I notice the time. Dax will be home in an hour from his shift guarding the store, and then it'll be my turn. The main island makes supply drops once a month and since there are no official police in Wolfsbane, the guys and I have taken up guarding things so no one gets any funny ideas about being in control.

I realize us guarding the food sounds like we might be trying to harness the power, but we don't deny anyone the things they want. We simply keep an eye on what is brought in, what's taken, and ensure no one hoards the supplies. We all need food. Wolfsbane used to be inhabited by ritzy shifters with ridiculous amounts of money and a somewhat surprising desire to use solar panels. Almost every house has them on the roof, and it keeps the electricity running. Granted, we have to use it more sparingly in the colder months, but it's a hell of a lot better than it could be.

Before I ended up here, I heard rumors of islands with no infrastructure at all.

Shit luck for those rejects.

"We know she was hurt." I point my beer at him. "She didn't kill George. And her name?"

He shakes his head. "Didn't hear it." Ripping off his damp top, he tosses it on the floor.

Staring at it for a beat, I wait for him to realize he's screwed up before freaking out. There are some things about living with other guys that drive me crazy. The general disregard for how messy they are is probably my biggest pet peeve.

"Chill, Ronan. I'll pick it up in a second." He groans and scrubs his face. "We don't even know who killed George."

"True, but there will be an investigation."

"Don't hold your breath," Creed mutters.

He jumps off the counter, bends to grab his shirt, and shoots me a serious look.

"That woman is going to be trouble. We should stay away from her."

"Should we?" I ask with a smile, aiming to piss him off. It works like a charm because he flips me off before storming out of the room and to the bathroom in the hall.

He slams the door shut like a petulant child, and I sigh and take another drink.

"Five minutes!" I shout, reminding him of the time limit on the hot water. We may have unlimited water, but the electric water heater uses a ton of our solar energy. Usually, we take cold showers, but Creed is soaked from the rain and probably cold.

The old pumping station is another responsibility we've taken on in our quest to make this place a home. Dax had to teach us a few things about maintenance, and we still need his help if something goes wrong, but at least we're learning.

Going back to my game of solitaire, I stare at the rows of cards, but I can't seem to focus on where to place the next one. All I can think about is the woman crazy enough to punch a guard in the face.

Trouble indeed.

seven

BELLATRIX

I make it to the kitchen as the water begins to boil in the teapot on the electric stove. She looks up from the glass container filled with dried leaves, pausing mid-scoop and glances over me. "The clothes fit."

"Yeah. You have tea?" I point to the jar.

Wow, look at us in our awkward conversation. This is why I despise trying to make new friends, you have to stumble through the first few encounters like an idiot until you figure out if you actually like the person or if you need to hightail it out of there and find someone more suited to your personality. For me, it's usually the latter because I'm a peach once you get to know me—read: sarcastic asshole.

Harlow nods, going back to filling a cloth bag. "The family who lived here before owned a tea shop. It's part of why I claimed this house. A garage full of teas and the supplies to steep it? My kind of place. I'm only missing a few types, but they usually send some in the supply drops."

"Hm. Are there any houses of former distillers? I do love tequila."

Moving to the breakfast bar side of the dark gray and black granite counter, I lean my arms against the back of the barstool.

"No tequila," Harlow says with an apologetic smile. "But I do know of a house full of beer. Pilfering it might be hard, but I think we can manage it."

My kind of woman. It may be a little early to say I like her, but hell, I like her.

"Cool. When do we leave?"

The change that comes over her face is instant. The happy spark in her gaze flickers out and her smile falls. She drops the tea bags into the mugs on the counter, grabs the teapot and switches the burner off, then pours the water over the leaves.

"You can't stay here."

Okay. I take back what I said.

"Do you want me to leave now?" The bite in my voice is sharper than I intended, and she lifts her eyes to meet mine.

"You can leave when the rain lets up."

"Fine," I snap, waving off the tea she tries to hand me. "I'll wait by the door."

"You don't have to do that." A hint of regret creeps into her words.

Rolling my eyes on the way to the foyer, I huff out a hard breath. Seriously. I made it all of ten minutes on the island before someone decided they didn't want me either? I've been trying so hard not to feel sorry for myself or sound like a baby, but I'm so tired and my muscles ache, so I'm not doing a good job of controlling my emotions.

Harlow follows after me, and I'm too close to freaking out to stay here. Honestly, I get why she might be hesitant to let me stay, but my heart can't take any more rejection. Grabbing my wet socks and shoes, I thank her for the clothes and run out of her house, leaving my wet ones behind.

"Bellatrix!"

I don't glance at her to see what she wants, she made it pretty clear I couldn't stay, and the rain has let up so now it's a light trickle. I can find my own way. She doesn't owe me anything, and I definitely don't want to be a burden.

The street is paved smooth, so the bottoms of my feet

don't hurt too bad from walking, and the water helps too. I start toward the bend in the road, really the only other direction I can go unless I want to start exploring the other houses on this loop. After the encounter with Harlow, I'm not in the mood to experience another warm welcome. My nerves can only handle so much.

I walk along the curb where the water is the deepest. The sewage system seems to work okay because a drain I pass is taking water as fast as it runs down to it, but there was enough moisture that there's a small stream flowing along the edges of the road. Thunder rumbles in the distance, threatening me. With a soft growl of frustration, I start walking faster. There has to be open shelter somewhere. A park, maybe?

Trees hug the road the farther I walk, creeping in close enough to feel a bit stifling. This island isn't exactly a forest, but the foliage is lush and thick, probably thanks to the rain and water surrounding it.

By the time I reach the end of the curve, the rain has stopped. My socks are dripping where I clench them in my hand. While I don't have a constant stream of water to cushion the ground, I continue to walk without shoes, holding them in my other hand. This is my only pair, and I don't want to destroy them any more than I already have.

Up ahead is a strip of stores on one side of the road, and a row of small beach-style huts across from them. The homes aren't nearly as fancy as Harlow's was, but they're still cute and welcoming. I eye the storefronts, wondering if the doors will be unlocked.

Seeing as there's no one around, it can't hurt to try.

Moving to the sidewalk, I cross the parking lot and go to the first store, peering into the windows. Most of the shelves are empty, but there are a few boxes of feminine products, toilet paper, paper towels, and other household products. No food though. I go to the next window, gasping when I see a wall of shoes. I glance up and read the sign above the store. *Island Feet.*

"Guess it's time to say goodbye." I stare at my shoes, twisting my mouth to the side. If anyone were around, I'd probably look absolutely insane.

But you know what? Who the fuck cares anymore?

Certainly not Harlow.

I drop the shoes and socks outside the door and try the knob. Locked. Of fucking course. It was too good to be true. Scowling, I yank the bobby pins out of my hair, frowning when I notice how flimsy they are. There are two grades of bobby pins: the kind that are short and made of weak metal that bends or warps easily, or the kind that seem like they're made of steel and could hold an updo in place for days.

Since these are the weaker kind, they're basically useless. I shove them back into my hair, pinning up the few strands that are a smidge too short for a ponytail. Turning, I scour the parking lot for a rock. There are a few bigger stones, but I don't want to make a huge mess, so I opt for the fist-size one I spot near one of the streetlamps.

"Ow, fuck," I mutter to myself. This parking lot is filled with random rocks and they dig into the bottoms of my feet.

Picking up my rock, I slowly walk back to the storefront, glaring at it like somehow it personally offended me. Lining up with the door, I take a step back so I can give it some oomph, and then swing my arm back.

This glass is mine.

Bringing my arm forward, I grunt and put my back into the throw. The rock sails through the air and a crazed grin spreads over my face as I watch it hit the pane, only, it doesn't shatter like I expected. The rock drops to the ground with a thud and a small chip is all the evidence there is of my attempted break in.

"They make that look so easy in the movies," I murmur.

"Well, for starters, those windows probably aren't as thick as these. I guess when they built the little town, they made sure shifters couldn't break things," a voice, rich and deep like an eighteen-year aged bourbon, says from behind me.

I squeak, whirling around to face a fox. No. Not a literal fox. A silver fox.

My GOD.

Remember earlier when I mentioned I liked sex? The sentiment doesn't exactly mean I'm led by my vagina, but shit, if she wanted to lead me to him, I'm not going to fight her because *damn.* Even after being rejected, I can't deny he's fine. In fact, he might be just what I need to make me forget about *Chad,* the bastard.

His hair is trimmed short on the sides, a bit longer on top, and the natural brunette color is peppered with gray. He has a strong jaw, or what I assume is a strong jaw. The guy looks like Henry Cavil but a bit older and with tattoos covering him. They travel up both arms, hiding the rest of the image under the shirt sleeve. I start to study the art, but I've already stared long enough.

Lifting my eyes to meet his dark blue ones, I laugh. "Horrible idea. How am I supposed to break and enter now?"

Mirth swims in his gaze, and he runs his hand over the slight stubble covering his jaw. "That's against the law."

"Who's going to stop me?" I ask with a smirk, mustering up some of the woman I used to be before this morning happened.

A dark chuckle, a quick, heated perusal of my body, and an answering smirk have me stepping closer. "Me," he says. What I said about his voice being like bourbon holds true. It's rich and dark and intoxicating. His alpha nature curls around me, not oppressing like Garry's but still riddled with *you will bend the knee.*

"You?" I set my hand on my hip and shake my head. "Who died and made you king?"

Of course the alpha reject would take it upon himself to try and control things. I guess I can't escape pack dynamics on this moon-forsaken island.

"You're funny." He glances past me and to the store. "I'm not a king, but I am in charge of protecting the supplies, and I can't let you break in for a pair of shoes."

I frown, and he tips his head to the side, studying my face.

"But I can let you in so you can get what you need."

Instant suspicion narrows my eyes. "Why?" I rub at my sore wrists, but stop when his eyes follow the motion.

"Because it's my job." A frown tugs at his lips.

I scoff. "You said your job was to protect the supplies, not hand them out. I don't know who you are and I'm not comfortable owing you favors." No matter how hot or alpha he may be.

"The supplies are for everyone. I do protect them, but I also help people get inside the stores." He pulls out a set of keys from his pocket and swings them around his finger, lifting a dark eyebrow at me.

"Fine," I say, turning back toward the store. "But no funny business."

"Funny business?"

I wave my hand, hoping he'll forget I even said that because why the hell would I say something like that? For the love of everything chaotic, I swear I'm going insane. The taser must have done a number on me.

"What's your name by the way?" I ask over my shoulder.

"Dax." His dark blue eyes jump from my ass to meet my gaze, and not an ounce of shame fills them.

"I'm Bellatrix." The only people who call me Trix are my friends and family, and he's neither.

"The pleasure is mine." He walks past me, intentionally brushing his shoulder against mine, and smiles.

"I'm sure it is," I whisper to myself, taking advantage of the view.

There are two types of men. The men who let the pants wear them, and the men who wear the pants. Dax *owns* his jeans.

I bite my cheek, reminding myself that I shouldn't recover from my rejection by jumping this guy. The idea isn't half bad, though.

No.

If Bella were here, she'd be rolling her eyes and calling me ridiculous. My sister's face flashing in my mind is enough to sober my promiscuous thoughts, and I wait patiently for Dax to open the store.

He slips a key into the lock and twists the knob. "Wolfsbane Island's finest shoe emporium is now open for business."

"You're a real comedian." I go inside, ignoring the way my stomach tightens when I pass him and glance around. "At least there aren't any Crocs."

There's every style of shoe, or almost every style of shoe, you could want. I scan the rows of shelves, looking for something practical. High-heels aren't my favorite, and I can guarantee I won't need any cute wedges or sandals. No. Here on this island, I'll need comfortable shoes I don't mind getting dirty in.

"What's wrong with Crocs?"

"Why do you sound so offended? Those shoes are—"

"Comfortable, breathable, soft," he offers.

"If you say so." I chuckle and go to the wall with Vans. I'm more of a Converse-lady myself, but these will do in a pinch.

Oh moon. Being stuck on an island is a *pinch*? What the fuck is wrong with me? I am pretty sure I'm in denial or something, because this isn't a normal reaction. Then again, I don't envision myself crying at every turn when this is my new reality. Sure, maybe I'm avoiding the emotions I feel, but it's better than falling apart in front of a stranger. Especially if that stranger is Mr. Silver Fox.

"The maroon are my favorite."

I give Dax a look and snatch the dark navy pair. Then squint at him and slowly reach for the black pair. His eyebrows rise centimeter by centimeter, and by the time I've curled my fingers into the back of the shoes, they hit his hairline.

"Two?"

Nodding, I hold them at my side. "One for daytime, and one for night. Two pairs are essential."

"Really?"

He doesn't sound convinced.

"Absolutely. Look at my poor toes." I pout and slide a foot forward, letting him see how raw they are from my short walk.

His eyes slip down my body, taking in my shorts, lean legs, pausing on my ankle which I find rather curious, and finally landing on my toes.

This man has *no* right to be so manly.

"Fine. Take two. The socks are over there." When his eyes find my face, they're pinched, and he abruptly turns to wait outside for me to finish.

"Okay."

Do I feel bad for torturing the man? Eh.

Do I love having two pairs of brand-new shoes? Yes.

I have nothing, so I'm taking my joy where I can get it. I grab simple black ankle socks, because the no-peek ones are uncomfortable as hell and I'm not trying to impress anybody with my lack of sock showing.

Turning to head out, my gaze catches on a stack of shirts

by the register. The black shirt has a wolf decal and Wolfs-bane Island written across the front in a sprawling script. I take one, and check for any other things I might need in this store.

Sandals.

Hm. I eye my hoard, feeling a twinge of guilt for taking two pairs of shoes, and decide I'll come back for sandals another day when my hands aren't full. Besides, maybe he'll forget about the second pair of Vans by then.

"Would you like a bag?" Dax deadpans when he sees I also grabbed a shirt.

"Oh! Yes, if you have a reusable one that'd be great." I give him a shit eating grin.

He shakes his head and glances away again, suddenly growing serious.

Damn.

The people on this island are giving me whiplash.

I plop down and put on the socks and the black Vans, sighing in relief when I stand. "Are you in charge of housing too?"

Dax is studying the tree line, I follow his gaze, squinting when I don't see anything. He grunts and turns back to me with a frown.

"What?"

"I asked if you were in charge of housing too."

"No. No one is in charge of housing. Find an empty one and claim it."

"Harlow didn't take too kindly to me barging into her house. Can you tell me what houses to avoid at least? I'm not really a fan of having a pan swung at my face."

His eyes widen. "Did she hurt you?"

"No. She didn't want me in her house, which is under-standable. I did barge in soaking wet, and I got mud all over her tiles. She'd just mopped, so she was a little pissed." I tug on my shirt. "She gave me new clothes though, so that was nice."

"She talked to you?"

"Uh, yeah." I wrinkle my nose at him. "Why?"

"She doesn't talk to us."

"Is it because of the voices?" I tip my head to the side and study him. He doesn't seem crazy, but with the sudden switch from happy to cold, it wouldn't surprise me if he did hear voices.

"What?"

"You said *us*." I wait for him to catch up.

Sometimes it takes a minute.

The moment it dawns on him, he barks out a laugh and runs his hand over his beard, eyeing me in appreciation. "I live with two roommates. Harlow doesn't talk to us, as in, she doesn't talk to me or my roommates."

"Mmm. Well, that's painfully boring."

He presses his lips together to keep from laughing, so I take that as my cue to leave. He is trying hard not to like me, and I'm not sticking around to find out why.

"No tips on what houses to avoid?"

"Numbers one, three, fourteen, thirty-five, and fifty-one are taken. Oh, and don't go near house number four."

"Why not?" I ask, lifting an eyebrow.

"Trust me, you don't want to live in that house."

"If it were any other day, I'd make you explain. Thanks for the help." I nod at him and continue in the direction I'd been headed.

Dax is fun, but I can't let my desire to make connections cloud my judgement. We're all here because we were rejected, and we're all messed up. I need to find myself, find out more about the people who live here, and get settled before I try and make friends.

eight

DAX

Blonde hair snares my attention as she walks away.

Bellatrix.

I roll her name around in my head a few times, thinking about the interaction and how much I acted like a little boy. I'm forty-seven, so I'm well past my horny teenage years, but for some reason, seeing her and bantering with her had me hard as a rock. She seemed a little thrown when I left her in the store, but I wasn't about to stand there with my dick growing hard in my pants.

She doesn't look back like I expected, and a little frown tugs at my lips.

Maybe she wasn't flirting.

Have I really been here long enough to forget how that sort of thing works?

Am I really fretting over this interaction like a teenage girl?

Shit.

I need a beer.

Checking my watch, I see my shift has already ended. Bellatrix distracted me. Blonde hair, pretty blue eyes, and lightly tanned skin. God, she's hot. Checking my surroundings, I head toward house number fourteen, which is around the corner from the stores.

"New chick in town," Ronan says as he walks by. "Creed's all worked up about her."

"I saw her. Can't say I blame him. Watch your back, brother. We still have a killer on the loose," I say, casting a glance in his direction.

He stops walking and turns. "Should we warn her?"

"She's already had a shit day. Maybe we can wait until tomorrow?"

"What if she's next?"

I pinch my eyebrows together, look at the house which is only a few yards away, and groan. "Fuck. I'll go watch her."

"Stalk her, you mean?"

"Would you rather do it?" I ask, rolling my eyes. These guys are like family, but sometimes they annoy the shit out of me.

"Hell yeah, I would."

"No you won't," I say, jerking my thumb toward the stores. "Go do your shift, I don't trust you to keep it in your pants."

"You should worry about Creed, not me. He's the one who had a boner for her."

I grimace because so did I.

"Worry about yourself," is all I say. "I'll tell Creed I'll be back in the morning."

He flips me off before heading to the guard post, strutting his usual unhurried strut.

Fucker.

∼

BELLATRIX

Settling on home number twenty, because I like my space and don't feel like walking any farther, I eye the solar panels on the roof before I walk up the steps. I swing my gaze around the porch. There's a cute swing, painted white, and a rocking chair next to it. The windows aren't huge on the front side of the house, but there are enough that I know plenty of natural light will come in.

With the solar panels, provided they work, I'll be able to keep the place warm in the winter. The door is unlocked, so I let myself in. The layout is similar to Harlow's house, probably built by the same builder, but the decor is wildly different. A hippie exploded, did some twirls, and left behind a strong stench of patchouli. It overwhelms my heightened sense of smell, and my nose twitches in response before I sneeze.

No wonder no one wanted this house.

While it's cute, it's a lot to take in. The small table at the front is covered by a tapestry, dried flowers sit in a vase, and tiny buddhas are lined up in a row at the front. I run my finger over a little belly, hoping for some luck, and eye the bright blue and orange oriental runner.

A purple framed, hexagonal mirror hangs on a wall, and a dead ivy runs the length of the other side, killed by lack of water. Vibrant beads mark the end of the foyer, hanging from ceiling to floor.

Not exactly my style, but with a little fresh air, I can make it work. Parting the beads, I take in the moody eclectic living room, complete with another bright oriental rug and all black elephant statues, and head to the row of windows. I open all three, inhaling the musky scent of earth hanging in the air.

On the plus side, the house is pretty clean, so I do a quick dusting before searching for a vacuum. So far, I haven't found an issue with the electricity, which means the solar panels must be doing their job.

About an hour later, I've vacuumed the house and wiped down all the kitchen counters. I wring out the dish towel and hang it over the sink to dry and head back to the couch, plopping onto it and stretching. It's six at night, and I should probably figure out what to do about dinner, but I don't feel like getting up. Now that I've found a little comfort, it's almost like my body is finally shutting down after everything it's been through. I'm surprised I've been able to go on this long.

I'll worry about food tomorrow.

A LOUD CRASH OUTSIDE WAKES ME. I SIT, GLANCING AROUND the now dark living room. The clock on the wall shows it's eleven at night. I scrub my eyes then glance around again when I hear shuffling feet.

"Who's there?" I ask loudly, hoping it'll scare off whoever it is.

No one answers.

I run to the windows I opened earlier and slam them closed, flipping the locks and shutting the curtains. I wrinkle my nose when I smell patchouli in the air; will the scent never leave? Remembering there's someone creeping around, I grab a knife from the kitchen. Once I'm wielding the chef's knife, I turn on the lights in both rooms.

The sound came from outside, and as far as I can tell there are no strangers in the house, so I slowly make my way to the front door, listening for any indication of anyone waiting outside.

Pressing my fingers into the wooden doorframe, I lean my ear against the wall.

Silence.

Maybe this is some sort of island hazing?

Freak out the new reject. I'm sure everyone here is dying for something fun to do, and what better way to do it than torture the newbie?

I turn on the porch light, exhaling when it comes on

without issue. Rolling my shoulders a few times, I drag in a deep breath and rip the door open. I may have done my fair share of breaking and entering, but that was college and my ex and his friends had stolen a bunch of my stuff, so they deserved it. At least my sleuthing skills are being put to use. I slink onto the porch, gluing my back to the wall while my heart pounds in my chest. The knife is clutched in my hand at my side and my arm starts to tremble.

I'm freaking out.

Sneaking around to get your things back is one thing, but preparing to potentially stab someone is another. If someone is here to hurt me, they're going to regret it. The wounds on my wrists still smart, but the extended nap I took refreshed me. I should have shifted a long time ago to heal, but I didn't want to forget the pain so easily. That and if I heal those wounds, the only ones I have left to acknowledge are internal ones.

No thanks.

My chest is heaving, so I focus my mind. The key to calming down is to take steady breaths, controlling what you can when you feel out of control. Six counts in, six counts out. I do that a few times, pleased to find my heart and breathing slowing down. Now that I'm a little calmer, I side-step my way to the side of the house, hesitating a second with the knife at the ready.

A soft brush of clothes is the only thing I can hear, and they're not my clothes. Someone is around the corner of the wraparound porch. Motherfuckers. I step around the corner, pointing the blade at Dax, whose mouth drops open when he sees the weapon.

Swinging his arm up, he backs up. "It's okay. It's okay. I'm here to protect you."

"Oh, really? Because it seems like you're here to be a stalker, old man." I jab the knife in his direction. "Let me guess, the island has you feeling a little lonely so you decide to try and come take advantage of me?"

Silver Fox stalking me might be flattering if it weren't for the still stinging rejection from Chad.

"What? No," he says with an indignant huff. "Did I give you that impression?"

"It's hard to tell anything about a person off of one conversation." I eye him, wondering if he's being honest. "Why are you here?"

"To protect you."

"Seems like the only thing I need protecting from is you." I take two quick steps forward, smirking when he scrambles away from the knife.

"Bellatrix, I swear. I'm here on business. Nothing more."

I narrow my eyes at him, then point the tip of the blade at his junk. "I will hack it off if you do anything stupid, do you understand me?"

The one self-defense class I took may come in handy if he tries to attack me. He probably doesn't expect me to be able to hurt him since he's an alpha, but I can. Maybe not enough to incapacitate him, but he won't take me without a fight.

"Understood," he says between clenched teeth. "Can you put the knife down?"

A question, not a demand. Interesting. Perhaps he is being honest. Most alphas would command me to drop the weapon. I scan him once more, noticing his clothes from earlier are wrinkled and the faint shadows underneath his eyes. He's tired.

"Hmm." I wait another second before lowering it. "Why do I need protection?"

"Straight to the point then?"

I nod. "Seeing as I don't know you and don't trust you, yeah. Tell me why you think I need protection so much as to creep around my porch like a weirdo."

"I wasn't creeping."

"Oh, snooping around someone's porch at midnight isn't being a creep?"

"Well, when you put it like that…" he trails off and sighs, rubbing the back of his neck. "I wanted to wait to tell you."

I bring the knife back up, and he groans.

"Speak, now." I slowly ease forward, clutching the handle.

He still doesn't overpower me with his words. Letting me get close with the blade isn't smart, but he obviously doesn't think I'll hurt him. Or maybe he's confident he can disarm me before I can. Either way, he watches me with curiosity rather than wariness. He's not a bit concerned about me. I bristle at the thought and toughen my scowl. I can be intimidating.

Shaking his head, he glances to the side. "Someone was murdered yesterday."

Spluttering, I tighten my grip on the handle. "And you didn't think to tell me this earlier?"

Is this why Harlow kicked me out? Is she the murderer? Or did she just want me to be killed first?

Fucking shifters.

His gaze strays to my arms, which are still covered in the dark marks from the silver chains and handcuffs. "I figured you'd been through enough for one day. Why haven't you shifted to heal yourself?"

"None of your business," I say. "What happened to the body?"

"The guard came for it, but we don't know who killed George. That's why I'm here, to make sure the killer doesn't come for you."

I wave the knife around. "How do I know you're not the murderer?"

Screwing his face up in frustration, he shrugs. "I guess you'll have to decide if you can trust me."

"Fat chance of that." I don't know if I'll ever trust a man again. I take a few steps back. "You should go."

"Bellatrix, I don't feel comfortable—"

"Go!"

My shout startles him, and to my surprise, he doesn't snarl back. He dips his head, face contorted with frustration as he skirts around me with his hands up. I wish he wasn't being so nice, because I feel a little bad for yelling at him. Then I remember he didn't tell me about a murder and took it upon himself to sneak around. I follow him to the front of the porch, not lowering the knife until he's down the stairs and standing on the sidewalk.

"You shouldn't be left alone."

"I'm fine." I glare at him. "Don't forget what I said. I'll hack it all the way off." Swinging the knife down for dramatic effect, I make a thwacking noise.

I think I see his mouth twitch into a smile, but it's gone before I can check again. "Lock your door." He turns and heads down the street. I wait until he's out of sight before slipping inside and doing as he said.

Just my luck, being stranded on an island with a murderer on the loose. I guess there is something worse than being rejected: death.

nine

RONAN

I double-check my watch when I see Dax strolling by on his way home. He should still be watching Bellatrix, so I don't know why he's here. Climbing down from the small guard station, I jog out from the trees and make a beeline for him.

"Hey, what are you doing?"

He gives me a haughty look. "She doesn't want to be saved."

"She saw you?"

Grunting, he nods and glances away. "I tripped on her porch. She came out with a knife and threatened to castrate me."

I whistle. "Damn, dude. Sounds like my kind of woman."

"Shut up," he mutters.

His ego must be wounded. I'm a beta and that sort of threat wouldn't bother me, but for an alpha? He must be seething. Alphas don't like to be challenged, but the way his frown deepens the longer the silence stretches between us tells me he isn't mad at all. More concerned, which is strange considering the circumstances.

Maybe this woman is trouble after all.

"Why didn't you find a new place to post up and look out?"

Seriously, it's a little surprising he didn't think of that.

"Oh I did, but she wouldn't go inside until I left. I just came for a coffee."

"You think that's safe?" I look in the direction he came from. "She's vulnerable."

"Trust me," he says with a shake of his head. "There's nothing vulnerable about Bellatrix."

Raising my brow, I give him a once-over, scoffing when it dawns on me. "You're fucking kidding me. You too?"

"Shut up, Ronan."

I laugh and shove his shoulder, walking with him to the house. Most everyone is asleep now, so I'm not so concerned about people coming to take advantage of the store. In reality, we probably don't even need to guard the supplies, but Dax insists we do it so there won't be some big confrontation. It's smart, but time-consuming on our end.

"Man, she must be something else. Or is it because it's been a while? Maybe your hand isn't cutting it anymore? I told you man, all you need is a fleshlight—"

He growls and I dodge the fist he throws, cackling as I dance out of reach.

"Whoa there, sunshine. No need to get violent if fleshlights aren't your thing."

"I hate you." He ignores me the rest of the way to the house, and I continue to take jabs at him for already being affected by her.

I know we've all been here a while, but this is a new record. Harlow came about seven months ago and neither of them reacted like this. I was interested until she gave me a death glare that screamed *I will murder you.*

"Must be her boobs," I say to myself. "Boobs have always been my weakness. You're a boob man, right, Dax?"

He rips the back door open and marches to the coffee machine, filling up one of the to-go cups we've been washing and recycling for guard shifts.

"Ass," he says after a long sip.

"Well, it's no Starbucks, but the coffee isn't *that* bad." I shake my head and fill up my own cup.

"No, stupid. I'm an ass man."

"Oh." I chuckle. "That makes more sense. Well, you know what they say."

"What?"

I frown at my coffee, realizing I don't know what they say. "Never mind."

"You know, for a smart guy, sometimes you're pretty dumb."

"You know, for a dick, you sure are little," I shoot back, smirking when his eyes darken. We've known each other long enough that he doesn't get all alpha or growly at me. He does, however, get annoyed.

"Whatever. I'm too old for this shit. I'll see you in the morning." He's only ten years older than me, but sometimes he acts like he's seventy.

"Too proud to admit defeat?"

He walks out of the house, lifting his hand and flipping me off without bothering to look over his shoulder. "Don't die."

"I'll try not to. You either," I say, forgetting all about our joking.

There's a murderer on the loose, and I don't think George is the only reject who will end up dead.

BELLATRIX

Soft tweeting wakes me, and for a second, I have peace. Rolling over in my bed, I pull the comforter up, frowning when the texture is off.

Did I fall asleep in my sister's room?

Sighing heavily, I peel my eyes open, glancing down at the bed only to find I don't recognize any of it. I jolt up, not caring that the sheet falls away to reveal my naked body. Memories from yesterday rush through my mind. Chad. His dumb sneer. Me rejecting him only to be rejected too. The cuffs and chains. The angry marks on my arms are proof it's all true.

I'm stuck on a fucking island, have a stalker who might be a murderer, and Chad rejected me.

Well, maybe I'm not stuck. I'm not the best swimmer, but a little determination can go a long way. First things first. I shift, landing on all fours, letting the magic of the change heal my wounds. I've let myself suffer long enough, and I'll need every ounce of energy I can get. The wounds might slow me down, so they have to go. I revert back to my two-footed form. My wolf whines, but I can't let her frolic through the town right now because our current mission is to escape. I have no idea how far I'll have to swim, but I have to try.

I hold my arms up, inspecting the faint dark brown lines running over my skin. The shift healed the worst of the damage, but it seems I'm going to have permanent scars from the silver chains.

Fucking Garry.

If he were here, I'd rip his head off. Since he's not, I opt for punching a pillow a few times then go get dressed. The fridge is mostly empty, except for some expired condiments, a container full of leftovers that look more like straight mold, and a jug of turned milk. I find a box of granola bars in the pantry and grab two, inhaling them as fast as I can because they're also expired and a little dry, but any food is better than no food.

Grabbing a short glass from the cabinet, I fill it with tap water and take a sip, washing down my pathetic excuse of a breakfast. I contemplate waiting a little while to attempt my escape, but I've already wasted over twelve hours. Yesterday I'd been too exhausted and the taser zapped the last of my energy, but I feel a lot better now that I've shifted and slept.

Time to see if I can swim to the mainland.

∼

CREED

A few minutes after I trade shifts with Ronan, she marches by with a fierce look of determination set on her face. She doesn't notice I'm watching, and I'm pretty sure she doesn't know where the guard station is, so I allow my gaze to stay stuck on her. Blonde strands haphazardly thrown into a bun, a Wolfsbane t-shirt, and short shorts. It shouldn't be attractive, but I've been imagining women in my head for years now.

Harlow doesn't count because she scares the shit out of me.

Seeing her in all her hot mess glory almost has me groaning in frustration. If this is my life now, it's going to suck. Not only does Dax's presence torture me—he has no idea I'm bisexual, has never shown an interest in men, and is oblivious to my crush on him—now hers will too. When she suddenly starts sprinting, I stand from the folding chair and lean over the railing of the lookout tower wondering what she's doing. The road bends so I can't see her anymore.

"Fuck," I mutter, smacking my hand on the wood and climbing out of the little booth we built in the trees. It's nothing fancy, but it's a lot more comfortable than standing or sitting in front of the store. The trees provide much needed shade during the long shifts, and it allows us to see in almost every direction. Every direction but around the damned curve in the road.

Dax would be pissed if he knew I left, but curiosity is digging its talons into me, and I can't leave her alone.

I have to know what she's running from.

Starting off in a sprint, I move to the shoulder so my steps are muffled, though if she's listening close enough, she'll hear my approach. With my heightened sense of smell, I follow her around the bend in the road, then veer into the trees, frowning when I realize she's running straight toward the water.

She's trying to escape.

She has no idea about the high frequency sonar, but she's about to find out first hand how painful it is for shifters, and if she's lucky, and I find her in time, she won't drown. I skid to a stop when I see a bronze strip of skin and slip behind a tree so she doesn't see me.

After a few seconds, I glance around the trunk and watch her stand at the edge of the island. There's no beach on Wolfsbane, so she's standing at a small drop-off. The water is fairly shallow, probably only six-feet deep, but it'll still be enough to cover her head.

I wish I could say I was stronger and I didn't let my gaze travel over every inch of exposed skin, but I'm a weak bastard. I greedily feast my eyes on her flesh, noticing a small strip of white around her waist; maybe from a thong style swimsuit? Her ass is the same shade as the rest of her sun-kissed skin, so she's definitely been out in the sun nearly naked.

Part of me wants to make some noise so she'll turn around, letting me see those tits, but I stay quiet, taking my fill over her profile and backside. Maybe it's the years I've been here, or maybe it's just her, but I'm certain I've never seen a body so perfect. Shaped like an hourglass, her hips flare and supple love handles tease me with the prospect of something to hang on to.

Adjusting myself, I suck in a hard breath, reminding myself I can't be the island pervert. The way I occasionally check out Dax is bad enough.

Lifting her hands over her head, she crouches slightly and pushes off the ground, diving into the water. She's lucky she missed the rocks. I count the seconds until she surfaces, sighing when her head pops up and she lets out a sharp laugh.

Now that she's somewhat covered, I step out from behind the tree and walk to where she stood moments before. She's too distracted, staring across the water, and she doesn't notice my approach.

"You can't escape that way."

"Motherfucker," she says with a gasp, spinning in the water and scowling at me. "Oh great. Another stalker."

Frowning at that, I point to the water. "You can't escape that way. You'll drown."

She squints at me. "Who are you?"

"No one," I say. "You should come back."

"Why, so you can murder me?"

Ronan mentioned Dax had to explain the murder to her. I know better than to think her aura of distrust is wholly attributed to the killer on the loose. No.

Rejection has a way of damaging shifters, shredding trust and optimism.

"I'm not the murderer, but you're going to drown if you try to swim."

She shakes her head. "I'm strong."

"I never said you weren't. They have high frequency sonar in the water. It messes with our enhanced hearing, and if you get far enough out to hear it, you're going to get confused and you'll probably drown. It's happened to a few shifters."

"I don't believe you." She turns and starts to paddle farther into the water.

"Dammit! You'll drown, you stubborn woman!"

"Better drowning than being murdered in my sleep by *stalkers*!"

"I'm not stalking you!"

She stops swimming and looks at me over her shoulder. "Then why were you staring at me before I jumped in?"

Shit.

"I—"

"Whatever. Go stalk Harlow." Then she dives under the surface, swimming underwater a bit before coming up for air.

Looking at the sky, I grind my jaw and try to turn around. I should go back home and forget about her. I should let her find out the hard way. I should not strip out of my clothes and jump in after her.

I've never been good at following my instincts, so I undress and jump in, ignoring the glare she sends my way as I start to swim after her in the cool water. If it weren't for my supernatural body and the warm temperature outside, my teeth would be chattering. She picks up her pace, trying to outswim me, but I'm a little faster than she is, so I catch up to her before she hits the first buoy.

The warning zone.

She stops for a second and glares at me. "What are you doing?"

Giving her space, I stop a few feet away from her and tread water. "Come on, let's go back. I'm not lying to you. You don't want to keep going."

"Why do you even care?" she mutters, swimming past the buoy.

Truth is I'm not even sure why I care, but I do. I don't want her to drown, and for whatever reason, my mind is screaming at me to grab her and drag her back to safety even though that would cross too many lines.

Without thinking, I yell after her, "If you start to drown and I have to try and save you, I'm going to smack that ass."

She huffs. "You can try!"

A tiny smile tugs at my lips, and I swim after her a little slower than I did before. She's close to reaching the second buoy, and that's when things will get complicated.

ten

BELLATRIX

The charming and annoyingly handsome creep is still following me, rambling about how I'm minutes away from disaster, but so far, I don't feel anything. Was he lying to lure me back so he could kill me?

He doesn't look like a murderer, then again, neither did Ted Bundy. His pretty green eyes and dirty blond hair don't make him innocent.

Even beautiful people can be twisted.

Taking another long inhale, I dive under the surface and breaststroke past the second buoy.

Eminent danger my—oh.

A high-pitched pulsing sound hits me, making me cringe and stop mid-stroke. I clamp my lips together and kick up, but another pulse of sound, on a higher frequency than the last one crashes into me. My eardrums tremble, and I forget about keeping my mouth closed, releasing a silent whine into the water. Bubbles float around me as water fills my mouth, and I gag, slamming it shut and spitting it out.

I'm sinking, pretty quickly, and I can't tell how deep the water is. Before I can get my wits about me, another pulse ripples through the water. The vibration rattles my brain and makes my stomach roil. I stick my fingers in my ear to try and block the sound out, but it's no use. Remembering to kick, I try to make my way toward the surface, only to struggle to keep moving when another frequency rocks into me.

Water fills my mouth when I scream, and this time I swallow some of it, instantly coughing and trying to expel the liquid only to suck down more into my lungs. My body starts to thrash of its own accord, a desperate attempt to fight for survival. I push all my will into moving my limbs, but another wave of sonar slams into me, and I forget how to breathe, then remember when even more water fills my lungs.

Oh moon.

He wasn't lying.

I'm going to drown.

Strong arms wrap around me, tugging me back at a rapid pace. I'm still coughing and taking in more water than is probably safe. I want to tell him to leave me, to save himself because I won't die with a guilty conscience, but I can't. I can't do anything but cough, suck in more water, and cough again.

My mind is racing, and my fingers are still stuck in my ears when we surface. Water cascades off of me, and I gag, throwing up water and almost slipping back under, but hands catch my waist and keep me steady while my lungs force the water out. A palm cracks against my back, helping me cough up even more. I cover my mouth with my hands, noticing blood covering the fingers I had plugging my ears.

"Are my ears bleeding?"

"Stubborn woman," the creep whispers, sounding a little too concerned for a murderer.

Something hard brushes against my ass, and I groan between coughing.

"Are you seriously hard right now? I knew you were a creep," I wheeze, still not together enough to pull out of his arms and keep myself afloat.

"I told you that you would drown, but you didn't listen."

Is he ignoring me?

Rude. Then again, he is saving my life, so he can't be all that bad. My entire body sags, having coughed up all the water but now too tired to help him on the way back.

"Almost there," he whispers again. His hips don't come close to my body again, and I can't help but think he's intentionally trying not to touch me. "Ronan."

"Who's that?" I start to shiver, the cold water getting to me now that I'm not swimming.

"My friend. I need his help to get you out," he says softly. "Ronan."

"Well, he'll never hear you if you keep whispering," I mumble. "Can't be pretty and smart, I guess."

I think he laughs, but he does it so quietly it's hard to tell. I crane my neck to glance at him, seeing his head thrown back in what should be a loud laugh, but I can hardly hear it. Reaching up, I rub my ears with my hands. Muffled sound is all that I register, and I frown, holding my palms in front of my face. Blood is covering my skin.

"She's hurt, dude. Help me pull her out." Now I know he's shouting instead of whispering, and I start to get worried.

Why are my ears bleeding so much?

I need to shift to heal, which means I have to get out of the water. He starts to lift me, so I glance up and grab the hands which are reaching down for me, using my feet to climb up the short, rocky drop-off. As soon as I'm on the ground, I shift, landing on all fours and whimpering when the pain doesn't immediately subside.

I'm in more pain than I realized, so I collapse to the ground, resting my head on my paws and waiting for my other form to heal. The creep climbs out of the water, completely naked, but I can't even appreciate the defined muscles.

His mouth is moving, and I hear the faint sound of their words, but I can't understand any of it right now. My ears are throbbing, and I close my eyes, waiting the pain out.

A hand brushes over my neck a few seconds later. I peel an eye open, staring at the long-haired god standing in front of me. Such a shame he isn't naked too, because he's just as beautiful as the creep.

"—pick you up," he says.

I can't respond in wolf form, so I eye him as he moves to the side, scooping two arms under my stomach and lifting me with ease. My head spins when he turns and heads through the trees, and I'm forced to close my eyes so I don't retch all over him. His fingers dig into my fur, holding me securely enough I relax in his arms, wondering why they're being so nice to me.

Maybe they're murder partners? They kill together or something?

No. That's insane. They're being much too gentle to be killers.

RONAN

The soft whimpers escaping her wolf has my chest tightening. Creed said she got caught in the sonar traps, something he's experienced before. The only reason he managed to make it out is because he swam back as soon as the first wave of sound hit him. Apparently, she stayed there, getting hit over and over by the sonar.

She's lucky Creed was there to rescue her.

Otherwise, she'd be the second dead body in two days.

Creed comes out of the house, fully dressed now after running ahead to get the clothes and the couch ready for her.

"Wake up Dax."

"Already did," he says, holding the screen door open for me.

Dax storms in, hair in disarray and eyes dark. "What happened?"

Gently setting her wolf form on the couch, I cover her with the soft throw blanket and let Creed fill him in. Bellatrix is still awake, but her eyes are clenched shut. The sonar is meant to hurt, and the shift doesn't seem to have healed her much, which means she needs to return to her human form, letting the magic of the change take away more of the pain.

I kneel in front of her, rubbing the fur covering her neck to keep her calm. "You need to shift."

A whimper.

"No, you have to. If the first change didn't take away all of the pain, you have to do it again. It's the only way. I know you're hurt, but you need to do it."

Slowly, she lifts her head, staring at me with yellow eyes that seem to pierce through me.

I nod. "There's a blanket covering you. We can leave if you want?" Tipping my head to the side, I try to guess what she's thinking, but it's impossible to read her wolf. "We'll wait in the kitchen," I tell her, standing and grabbing the guys. "Let's give her some space."

I'm not worried about leaving her because I can see the couch from the open concept kitchen, but at least she'll have a little bit of privacy. Dax is glaring at Creed like he's done something wrong, so I point at him.

"Don't start. If it weren't for him, she'd be dead."

His face loses some of that hard edge, and he scrubs his hand over his scruff. "Why didn't you stop her?"

"I tried," Creed says, crossing his arms over his chest. "She wouldn't listen."

"You should have dragged her back."

"Dude," I mutter, shaking my head and pinching the bridge of my nose. "That's a horrible idea."

Dax swings his angry gaze my way. "Better than her almost drowning!"

"Uh, guys? I can hear you yelling now, and it hurts."

"Shit," Creed says under his breath, returning to the living room.

Dax and I stare at each other for a beat before shoving aside our frustration and going to check on her.

Creed is sitting on the edge of the couch, and she's pressed into the arm of the other side, studying him. The blanket is wrapped tightly around her body, but her legs peek out the bottom. Her skin is so soft.

"You're not the murderer?"

Creed's lips kick up, and he runs his hand over the back of his head. "No, I'm not."

"What about those two?" she asks him, not bothering to look at either of us yet.

Dax bristles, probably offended she's ignoring him, but I give her time. She's been through a lot, and I don't blame her for wondering since she doesn't know us.

"No, they're not."

Chewing on her lip, she thinks about whether or not to believe him, then nods. The wet strands of her hair are soaking through the blanket, but she's plenty covered. Her eyes lift from Creed, sweeping over Dax, and then moving to me. There's no mistaking the distrust, but her face softens a little when I smile at her.

"Hungry?" I ask, jerking my thumb toward the kitchen. "Dax makes a mean omelet."

"Bacon?"

"Always," I reply earnestly because what kind of monster makes an omelet without bacon?

"I'll get it started." Dax leaves the room like his ass is on fire, and I bring my eyebrows together, sliding my gaze back to Bellatrix.

She lifts a shoulder, telling me she also noticed how quickly he left but can't explain what crawled up his ass.

"Come on. I'll show you the shower. Creed can go to the store to get you some clothes."

He opens his mouth to tell me off but stops and thinks better of it. He's never liked being told what to do, but making sure she's comfortable is my top priority, and I think he realizes it's what is most important as well.

"Thank you." She stands, adjusting the blanket so it covers all of her, and I have to pull my gaze away before I stare too hard at the way it contours to her curves.

Boobs are dangerous.

eleven

BELLATRIX

The water heater in this house is magic, even so, I make sure not to stay under the scalding spray for too long because I don't want to waste it all. Someone came in and dropped off clothes, which was only a little awkward. The curtain is dark, and I'd rather have clothes than walk around in a towel, so I can't complain.

Turning off the water, I squeeze out my hair and snag the fluffy towel off the hook on the wall, drying myself before twisting my hair in the towel to let it dry. I pick through the small stack of clothes, grabbing a thong and trying not to think about why Creed, the creep who saved my life, went with the slinky underwear. There are a pair of jean shorts which are a little too big but fit well enough they don't fall off. There's no bra. I'm not sure if that was intentional or an oversight, so I tug on the tank top, frowning at how my nipples show through the material.

Bastard.

Whatever, I'm not ashamed of my boobs, and if he wants to torture himself by bringing me a shirt without a bra, he can suffer. I undo the towel on my head and scrub my hair a bit before finger combing it, settling it in a mostly neat style. It'll be a bit frizzy when it dries, but my hair is straight enough it won't look too bad.

I search the cabinet drawers for an extra toothbrush, but come up empty. I contemplate using one of theirs, but think better of it. No telling what sort of germs they have. Shifters can't get diseases like humans, and we don't get sick, but I don't know them nearly well enough to share a toothbrush. So, I use my finger, cleaning my teeth as well as I can.

After I rinse and spit, I study myself in the mirror, knowing I'm stalling. My blonde hair is mostly tangle free, but I can only do so much without a brush. Ultimately, the smell of frying bacon drags me out of the safety of the bathroom. I pad down the hall, trying to listen to their hushed conversation. My ears have healed enough I can almost make it out, but there's still a little damage. I'll shift again later to heal the rest of the way, but for now, I want food.

My stomach growls in agreement, and I tip my chin up, strutting into the kitchen like I belong in their house and putting my hands on my hips.

"If any of you try to kill me, I'll castrate you. Capisce?"

Ronan bites his bottom lip, trying not to laugh, and Creed's gaze slips down my body, oblivious to the threat hanging in the air.

Dax turns, pan in hand, and scoffs. "You sound like Harlow, only less threatening."

I'm plenty threatening, so I have no idea what he's talking about.

"Try me, Old Man."

He gives me a dark look. "Your food is ready."

"Oh. Thanks." I meet him at the counter, watching as the giant omelet slides out of the pan and onto my plate without any help.

The eggs are perfectly cooked, and I think I see bell peppers or tomatoes. He definitely can't be the murderer because I'm going to need one of these again. Ignoring the weight of their gazes on me as I take the plate from Dax, I go sit between Creed and Ronan.

Creed stiffens, back going rigid, and I smirk, settling in like nothing about this is weird. I catch Ronan's eyes, which are a reddish-brown color, and he releases a soft laugh when he sees my grin. Dax leans his hands on the other side of the counter, intently watching me take my first bite. I hold his stare, wrapping my lips around the fork and savoring the flavor.

"Oh, man," I mumble around the food, nodding my head and pointing to the plate. "This is good shit."

His eyes light, and the answering smile I get almost makes me choke. "Coffee?"

"Definitely," I say around another bite. "One scoop of sugar, please."

"Well, when you ask so nicely." He turns to the coffee pot, filling up a mug for himself and then for me, scooping a generous heap of the glorious white granules.

Sugar and caffeine, the only legal forms of crack. Not that shifters get much of a rush, it's more about the ritual than anything. Something about drinking a warm cup of coffee brings me comfort.

I continue eating, blocking them out because if I focus on how aware Creed seems to be of my proximity or the way Dax and Ronan study me without a care in the world, I'll get nervous. I'm a confident woman, but they're unreasonably attractive, and I almost died because I ignored Creed's warning. Then there's the whole dragging me out of harm's way while being completely naked part. I'm not immune to embarrassment, but I can fake all the confidence in the world if I have to.

Fake it till you make it, folks.

Taking a sip of the coffee, I hold back a grimace much to Dax's amusement.

"Wolfsbane's finest brew." He lifts his cup. "Apparently, the High Pack doesn't think we deserve the good stuff."

I pull the cup back, giving it a suspicious look but deciding to drink it anyway. "So they bring supplies?"

Dax nods. "They make drops once a month."

"Hmm. At least they bring us food." I finish the last of the omelet and push the plate away, resting back in my seat.

"That's all they bring." Creed side-eyes me, gaze slipping down to my chest before snapping back to my face.

I put my arms under my boobs and push them up a little, mocking him. He's the idiot who brought me a tank top, may as well make him pay for it.

Ronan chuckles again, and I tip my head in his direction.

"You all live together?"

He nods. "Yup."

"How many people live on the island?"

"Counting you? Ten."

I eye his long hair and beard, wondering what they feel like. "Minus the dead body?" I ask, relishing in the way his mouth pops open in surprise.

"Yeah," he grunts. "Minus the dead body."

"Do you have any suspects?"

"The guard is going to investigate," Dax begins, but Creed's growl cuts him off.

"They're not going to do shit, you know that."

I watch the men have a silent conversation, wondering what the stewing looks and lifted eyebrows mean.

"So that's a no," I say, tapping my fingernails on the counter. "Thanks for breakfast. Who's going to let me into the store to get food?"

"You're leaving?" Creed sounds betrayed.

I roll my eyes. "Yes, as much as I loved the omelet, I'm ready to go."

"You don't have to leave," Dax says, grabbing the plate from the counter and taking it to the sink. "Are you still in pain?"

"A little, but I'll survive." I look at Ronan. "Take me to the store."

He seems like the safe bet.

"Let me grab my keys." He ignores the glares Dax and Creed shoot at him and runs up the stairs, likely going to his room to get what he needs.

"Bellatrix, it's not safe."

"Call me Trix," I correct before I think better of it.

Creed nods. "Okay. Trix. You should really stay here."

"I'm good. Besides, isn't Harlow in danger too? I don't see you asking her to stay with you."

"Harlow is a different story."

I give Creed a look. "How?"

No one answers me.

"Cool. I don't want special treatment because I almost died. I'll be fine."

"Ready?" Ronan asks when he returns, resting his hip on the wall and twirling the keys around his fingers.

"Thanks for breakfast." I smile at Dax then cut my gaze to Creed who still looks ready to argue with me. "Thanks for saving my life, but don't think I forgot about you perving on me."

His cheeks turn scarlet, and my stomach does a little flip. Now is not the time to listen to my insatiable libido. I hop out of my seat and strut out like I don't have a care in the world, including a nip-slip. This shirt is really tight, but I kind of like the way Creed looked at me.

No, Bellatrix. You can't go there.

Here's the thing, I know what I should and shouldn't do, but I have a little demon who whispers *why the hell not* all the time, and I have a tendency to listen to the fucker.

I'M IN THE MIDDLE OF GRABBING SOME LUNCH MEAT WHEN Ronan pops up beside me. His smile is wolfish, and I side-eye him.

"What?" I drop the turkey into the basket I'm carrying and go to find bread.

He trails after me, clicking his tongue. "You've made quite the ruckus with my friends, you know."

"Oh?" I lift an eyebrow at him.

Grabbing the whole-wheat loaf, I move to the snack aisle. Technically, I should be more concerned about fruits and vegetables, but chips and salsa are essential for a healthy diet. I think my doctor told me that.

"Mmhmm. I've never seen Creed blush so hard or Dax be so willing to serve."

I shrug. "What can I say? I have a way with men."

"I bet you do, Trix." The way he says my name, deep and tempting, has me swinging around to face him. His eyes skate over my body and he nods, a piece of brown hair falling out of his man bun. "Yup. He was right."

"Who was right and what about?" I cock my hip and tap my finger against my side, holding the basket with my other arm.

"Creed. He said you were trouble."

"Is that so?"

"Yup."

"Well, seeing as I have no plans of being around you all, you don't have to worry about little old me."

"That's a shame."

I glare at him. "Are you flirting with me? I almost died like an hour ago."

"But did you die?"

"Jerk," I mutter. "I could have."

He tips his head back and forth. "Probably, but you didn't. You know you can stay with us though, right? I'm sure Dax and Creed would be thrilled."

"You sure are doing a lot of talking for them. What about you?"

"Me?" he asks, rubbing his hand over his beard.

"Yeah." I step closer, noticing the faint flecks of gold in his irises. "How would you feel about me moving in?"

"It wouldn't bother me."

I try not to frown. It wasn't the fun sort of answer I was expecting, but he's being honest. A slow smile crawls over his face.

"Not what you wanted to hear?"

"It's not not what I wanted to hear." I grab a box of white cheddar Cheez-its and a bag of chips. "I'm done."

"I'll grab you a bag," he says, surprising me again when he doesn't continue to pester me about what I actually wanted to hear. He's perceptive, but he's not going to be an asshole about it which I appreciate.

Meeting him at the counter, I set the basket down and help load the items into two reusable bags. He doesn't say much as we work, and when my basket is empty, he holds up the straps for me to grab.

"I'd offer to help you, but I think you might tell me to get fucked."

I laugh and nod. "You're probably right." Taking the bags, I tip my chin up. "You're not so bad. Thanks for the help."

Then I leave him to close the store and start back toward my home... or at least, the house that I've claimed. This island isn't home. It's essentially jail but without cold metal bars and shit food.

Since I can't escape, I'll have to find a way to be comfortable here. Which means no matter how much I hate this place, it is my new home.

This is the worst.

twelve

CREED

A few days pass and we don't see much of Trix. We still watch her house every night because we have no leads on the killer and everyone else on the island is acting strange. Since there are only nine of us that were here when George was killed, and the guys and I are ruled out, that's six suspects. Too many for my liking. As I thought, the elders don't give a shit about what happened and no one has come to investigate.

I lean against a tree trunk, staring at Trix's windows, hoping to see a glance of her. Creep. She called me a creep, and given how desperate I've been to be around her, she's not entirely wrong. I've been picturing her in that tiny tank top way too much, and my cock is aching for attention. There are only so many cold showers I can take before I have to take matters into my own hands—literally.

Dax insisted we rotate watch like we do the guard shifts, and tonight is my first night. I am entirely unprepared for the flash of skin I see through the side window. I crouch down, resting my chin against my hand and watch as she struts around in nothing but the tiny top and a pair of skimpy underwear.

"Damn," I mutter. It's like she is intentionally trying to rile me up, but she doesn't know I'm here, or she shouldn't if I've done my job right.

My shorts get uncomfortably tight with my erection

pressing against the zipper. I run my hands through my hair, trying not to stare at her perky ass. Or those pretty tits in her top, or her—fuck. I'm not going to be able to stop watching now that I can see her. She looks like she's singing, and the way she shakes her hips tells me she found some music. Since I know where she is, and that she's safe, I don't see why I can't work off some of this frustration.

I kneel down, undo my zipper, and grab my dick, biting back a moan when I stroke it and rub my thumb over the head. My hand doesn't feel nearly as good as the real thing, but it'll have to do. If anyone were walking by, they'd be able to see me thanks to the streetlights, but I'm counting on that not happening. Everyone has been staying inside since George's death, not that we had big parties or anything before that.

This is the first time I've had someone to watch while I jerk off, so I greedily stare at her ass, watching her bounce around the room while I slowly stroke myself, drawing it out. I pick up the pace, not bothering to silence my moan, and close my eyes as I start to get into a rhythm. The area surrounding the house even smells like her, and I bite my lip, concentrating on her scent and pumping my fist. The next time I open my eyes, she's gone. I frown but don't stop because I'm so fucking hard, and I hate blue balls.

Leaves crunch to my right, so I stop and glance around. No one is out here. It must have been a squirrel or something. I lean my head back against the tree trunk, pumping my hand up and down my shaft faster and faster.

"What do we have here?"

Her voice scares the shit out of me, and I pull my hand from my dick, holding them up like she's a cop pointing a gun at me and I'm trying to prove my innocence. She steps out from behind a tree, a smile tugging at her lips as she glances me over. My cock is still hard, and it twitches when her gaze strays in that direction. Her throat bobs, and she steps closer.

"What are you doing out here, Creep?"

"My name is Creed." I swallow when I see she's still in her top and underwear. This chick is wild.

She hums, taking another step all the while keeping her attention on my erection. Her lack of clothing is rather distracting, and I can't help but flit my gaze to her thick thighs. I can't wait to bury my face between them.

"Pretty sure it's Creep." She squats down a foot in front of me, finally lifting her eyes to meet mine. "Is that for me?" Gesturing to my cock, she bites her lip and furrows her brow like she's confused.

"I-" Hell, what do I say to that question? "Yes."

"Well then," she says, dropping to her knees and scooting closer. "Let's take care of that." She runs her manicured finger up my thigh.

My muscles jump in response and my hips thrust forward, practically begging for her help. She chuckles, but I'm not ashamed. Anything is better than my hand. She cups my balls, tipping her head to the side and staring into my eyes.

"Are you going to ask nicely, Creep?"

Fuck. I'm not even mad at the stupid nickname, especially not when she gently tugs on my nuts. "Yes, fuck. Please."

"Please what?" she asks, leaning close enough to kiss my jaw. "What do you want?"

"Fuck," I mutter, because this is weirdly hot as hell and she's asking me what I want. I try to think of something sexy to say, but I come up short.

"If that's what you want, you'll have to come inside." She withdraws her hand and stands, brushing her knees off.

I scramble to stand and yank my pants up. She's already

halfway to the house by the time I catch up with her, and she casts a wink over her shoulder.

"I've always wanted to sleep with a stalker."

"I'm not a stalker," I say.

"You were watching me through my window."

"To keep you safe." I open the back door.

"And keeping me safe includes jacking off?" She stops next to me and gives me a sultry smile.

Well shit. Instead of trying to reason away my actions, I shrug and hold the door for her to pass through.

"What else was I supposed to do when you're dancing around like that?"

She grins at me, grabs my arm, and drags me to the bedroom I'd been watching her in. I stumble along with her, wrinkling my nose at the faint scent of patchouli hanging in the air, but when she stops in front of the bed and turns to me, I forget about the hippie smell.

"Drop the shorts." She rips her shirt off, freeing her breasts.

I think my brain short-circuits because when she hooks her fingers in the top of her underwear, she gives me a look.

"On it," I say like an idiot, taking them and my boxers off before tugging my shirt over my head.

She whistles in appreciation and steps closer, pressing her chest against mine. Fuck, her body is so soft. I grab for her, but she smacks my hands away with a tsk.

"What's the magic word, Creep?"

"Please," I say, hating how raspy my voice sounds.

"Good boy."

BELLATRIX

I run my palms over his abs, loving every inch of muscle and how they tighten in response to my touch. I hadn't planned on torturing him, but when I noticed him out there earlier, part of me couldn't resist.

Perhaps I'm playing with fire, but I've learned to love the burn. If I'm stuck on the island for the rest of my life, I'm taking what I want, and I won't feel ashamed for wanting sex or liking how Creed responds to me being near. Besides, he's kind of cute when he's flustered.

He's standing with his hands clenched at his sides, trying so hard to obey even though I know it's killing him. I grab his arms and slowly step to the side, turning him so his back is facing the bed. Going on my toes, I trace my tongue over his lips, tasting them before I press my mouth to his. He starts to reach for me, but I put my hands flat against his chest and shove him onto the bed.

His emerald eyes widen in shock, but he recovers as soon as I climb over him, settling my hips over his. I grin when he sucks in a hard breath, and I roll my hips so my slit slides over his length. He bites back a moan.

"Hey, Creep?"

"Yeah?" he asks in that sexy rasp of his.

"Touch me."

Without further encouragement, one of his hands grabs my ass and the other one goes straight for my clit. For a while there I had him pegged for a virgin, but I sincerely doubt that now. His thumb swirls over the sensitive bundle of nerves, pressing down when I roll my hips forward again.

"Fuck, you're so hot."

I laugh. "You too, Creep." Capturing his mouth again with mine, I kiss him while he teases me.

Our kisses aren't poetic. They're desperate and hungry and raw. Just the way I like them. Too much sweetness makes me cringe, and I don't think I could handle some swoon-worthy romance right now. The bond breaking hurt like a bitch, but it could have been worse. Since it had just been initiated, it didn't get too deep. I escaped the rejection in relatively good shape, aside from some minor scarring.

"Hey, where'd you go?" he asks, pulling back from our kiss.

I glance at Creed, grimacing. "Sorry."

"Do you want to stop?"

"And waste this perfectly good cock?" I roll myself over his length again and shake my head. "Hell no."

Before he can say anything else, I grab the back of his neck and bring his lips to mine. He moans into my mouth when I move my hips enough that the head of his dick brushes my center.

"Tell me what you want," I demand, breaking away from the kiss and trailing my mouth down his jaw and neck, biting his pulse point. I'm not sure what it is about him, but for some reason, I need to hear him say it. I want to hear him beg me for my pussy.

"I want to fuck you."

"Mmhm." I circle the head of his cock, teasing him at my entrance. "What else?"

He thinks for a second, his eyebrows lowering in the cutest way, so I kiss his jaw again.

"Say it."

"I want your pussy around my dick."

Ding, ding, ding.

"Good boy." I grab him and slide down until his shaft is all the way in me, stretching my walls and filling me up. He throbs inside of me, and I rock my hips once, watching when his nostrils flare in response.

"Put your hands here," I grab them and place his palms at the back of my hips, "and squeeze."

He listens, gently gripping my love handles. I circle my hips, working up his length and then back down, watching him try to keep control of himself and failing miserably.

"Harder," I say, holding his hands with my own and leaning back to ride him.

"Fuuuuck," he says, grabbing me with the right amount of pressure this time.

I stop messing around and ride him like I'm trying to prove my worth, like my life depends on it, and like my body wants me to. Trailing my hands up my body, I grab my boobs and pinch my nipples, grinding down hard on him.

He releases a growl and grabs my hips, flipping me over. My back hits the mattress and he holds on to the headboard, working me over with slow, hard thrusts that make the bed shake. He hits my G-spot and my toes tingle, curling slightly as he hammers into me.

"Oh shit," I mutter, wrapping my arms around him and lifting my hips to meet his. "Oh. Shit."

"Come on, girl, give it to me."

He pulls almost all the way out of me before slamming in so hard my mouth drops open and I choke on a moan. He does it again, and I dig my nails into his back, crying out when he picks up his pace and keeps battering my pussy with his thick cock.

"Right there, baby, let me hear it. Scream my name." His mouth finds my neck, but instead of kissing me, he bites down.

My entire body lights with fire, and I come all over him, shamelessly soaking the sheets and shouting his name between gasps. He kisses my tender skin and thrusts one more time, staying deep inside me while his hips jerk with his release. I hook my ankles around his waist, keeping him in and gently moving my body to take all he has to give me.

"Damn, Trix."

I let out a throaty chuckle and kiss his shoulder, then his neck, and finally claim his lips with mine.

"You're not so bad yourself, Creep."

thirteen

BELLATRIX

Creed and I jolt awake the next morning at the same time, furrowing our brows at one another and wondering what the hell woke us.

Then we hear it.

A scream.

It's faint, so the person must be far away, but there's no doubt someone is hurt. My eyes widen and I cover my mouth, shaking my head.

"Stay here," he says, "I'll go see what's going on."

"Like hell! You can't go out there alone! What if the murderer is out there?"

"I thought you thought I was the murderer?"

"I changed my mind."

Unless you count murdering my cunt… no, fuck. Trix. Now is not the time for jokes, someone might be dying.

"I'm coming with you," I say, deciding for the both of us. Tossing on the shorts, shirt, and shoes I wore yesterday, I rush out of the house after Creed.

His head swings back and forth, searching for danger. "The screams are coming from the water."

He starts to run, and I don't need to be told to keep up. I match his pace, dashing through the streets and sprinting toward the dock where I was dropped off. Dax is already there, and so is Harlow. Her eyes are red-rimmed and she falls to her knees about the time Creed and I run down the wooden planks.

"What happened?"

Dax gives a grim shake of his head and turns back to the water.

Following his gaze, I gasp when Ronan's head pops up, breaking the surface with a hard gasp. His hair is tied back, but with the water weighing it down, some pieces have slipped out. He flicks his head to the side so he can see and huffs out a breath. In his arms is a man I don't recognize. I haven't met any of the other island occupants, but I've seen a few pass by my house.

"Is he okay?" Harlow croaks, clutching her chest.

Creed doesn't hesitate to dive in the water fully dressed. He swims to his friend and together they bring in the man who hasn't moved since Ronan surfaced. Before Ronan can say the words, I know he's dead.

"He didn't make it." Ronan and Dax share a look while Creed starts to do CPR.

Harlow's sobs fill the air, and I watch with a strange sense of detachment as Creed's palms pump against the stranger's chest. He doesn't seem to notice the man's veins, which are raised and a funny shade of silver. This man didn't die because he drowned. Someone poisoned him.

Curses fill the air, and I don't know who is shouting, because all I can focus on is the way the man's chest responds to the pressure. A sharp ringing fills my ears, and I sink to my knees, watching the failed attempt to save a life break Creed.

His face is red, and his jaw works as he continues to try. Dax squats down and snaps his fingers in front of his friend's face, but Creed doesn't react. Harlow pinches her eyes shut, and she sways back and forth.

Ronan and I lock gazes, and his eyes mist a little. Unlike most men, he doesn't look away so I can't see the tears. He wears them like war paint, and I nod, understanding without him needing to say a word.

We're not safe. We're not wanted. And ultimately, we're alone.

He breaks our connection and goes to Creed, grabbing him around the middle and hauling him away from the man. Thrashing and reaching for the shifter, Creed tries to break away to continue, but Ronan holds fast. The wild look in Creed's eyes hurts my heart.

Dax growls when he lifts the dead man's wrist, eyeing the veins. "Fuck." He sets the arm down and drops his head, locking his fingers on the back of his neck and screaming, "Fuck!"

With a flinch, Harlow snaps her mouth closed, trembling in fright.

"Harlow," I say, holding my hand out for her, but she snaps her head in my direction, looking like a deer caught in headlights.

A soft whimper passes her lips and she jumps up, sprinting to her house and away from us. I watch her go, lines wrinkling my forehead.

"What happened?" I ask softly to no one in particular.

"I heard him screaming from the guard tower. Harlow and I got here at the same time, but we were too late. He'd already gotten to the second buoy." Ronan is still holding Creed, who is now subdued and staring at the lifeless body on the dock.

"He didn't drown," I say, pointing to his arms. "That's silver poisoning." Silver nitrate is one of the few things that can fatally wound shifters, but I don't need to tell them that.

Dax drops his hands from his neck and scrubs his hands over his eyes. "Creed, take Trix home. Ronan and I will deal with the body."

Creed is a beta, so Dax's command should snap him out of whatever he's feeling and thinking, but I can see his struggle, his willingness to fight Dax's authority. Despite being told to take me home, I rise from my knees and hook my arm in Creed's, leading him back to his house so he doesn't start something.

How did this day start out so shitty after such an amazing night?

~

DAX

As soon as Trix and Creed are out of sight, I pick up Seth's hand and study the silver lines on his wrist. Ronan squats on the other side of his body, and I lift my gaze to meet his.

"We have a problem."

I grimace and glance around, eyes shooting to Harlow's house. She got here at the same time as Ronan, but she should have made it before he did. Unless she was trying to cover her tracks.

"Harlow?" he asks, guessing what I'm thinking.

"I don't know," I confess. "She seemed shaken. All the true crime documentaries I've watched say that the killers usually don't react that way."

"Well, it's the only lead we have." He sighs and glances in the direction Creed and Trix went.

"He'll be okay. You know why this is hard for him."

Creed was preparing to apply to med school when he got rejected. George's death didn't hit him as hard because there was no way he could be saved, but with Seth, there was a chance. Or there would have been if he hadn't been poisoned.

"I'll go get the flare gun," Ronan says, slapping his thighs and storming toward where we keep the supplies in the shed at the end of the dock.

Since we don't have phones, the only way to get the

guard's attention is to shoot off a flare or flag them down. I frown and stare across the water. I was sure they'd send someone after George, but it's almost been a week and no one has shown up. I guess Creed was right: they don't give a damn.

If they won't help us find the murderer, we'll have to do it ourselves.

fourteen

BELLATRIX

After he changes into dry clothes, I sit next to Creed on the couch, picking at a loose thread and biting my cheek. He hasn't said a word since Dax ordered him to take me home, and I'm not sure what to say to him. 'It's not your fault' sounds stupid, so I settle for sitting with him until he's ready.

When I tug the string free, his hand brushes against mine. I slip my palm into his, linking our fingers and turning to face him. I lean my head against the back of the couch, holding his gaze.

"Do you want to talk about it?"

His face contorts, like he's in physical pain, and he shakes his head.

"Okay." I nod, feeling like an idiot. "Can I tell you a story instead?"

"Yeah," he says, voice hoarse from all the yelling he did.

"Once upon a time there was a beautiful woman. Her mate was an omega and got bullied a lot. The woman was a delta, and while she could defend him to a point, she couldn't stop him from getting hurt or beaten. One day, she came home from work to find her mate lying on the porch. He wasn't moving, and for a moment, the woman thought he might be dead." I swallow, blinking a few times to clear the tears. "But he wasn't. He was beaten within an inch of his life, but his heart still beat."

I remember hearing my mom's screams from across the

pack's land. I'd been on a walk with Bella when the cry rose through the air, the sound violent and broken all at once. My sister and I shared a look before shifting and racing home, dashing around the other members of the pack who heard her and came to see what was happening.

I'll never forget how pale her face was or how wild her eyes were, like she'd challenge any wolf, even the alpha, if they tried to talk to her or take him from her arms. It took Bella and me a few minutes to get her to agree to let the healer come help. Shifters can heal on their own if they shift, but healers can provide tonics or balms for any lingering scars and pain. They can also help most shifters shift if they're too weak to do so on their own.

His forehead creases, but I continue the story, skipping over the gritty details and hoping it'll distract his mind.

"So she found her family a new home. Her two daughters followed them across the country, even though they were both fully grown, to a pack they thought would treat their father kindly."

I take a deep breath and look away, wrinkling my nose as I continue and trying not to let the pang of longing in my chest make me cry.

"Well, when they arrived, the oldest daughter met her fated mate."

"He was an idiot," Creed interjects, guessing the rest of the story.

"Maybe." I shrug. "Apparently, if you're not a virgin, you're tainted goods." A bitter laugh passes my lips. Try as I might, I can't get over that fact. Chad should mean nothing to me, but because he is, or was, my fated, the rejection still stings.

A soft growl rises in Creed's chest, and I squeeze his hands.

"Trust me, I want to rip his dick off as much as you do, but we're stuck here."

"You're not tainted." His entire face softens, and he stares at me long and hard, begging me to hear him.

I nod, smiling at him. "I know," I say, but even still, my eyes fill with tears.

Despite trying to pretend like it doesn't bother me, being rejected made me feel like the only thing that mattered was how sacred my vagina was. That's not what I imagined my fated mate would care about, and it's kind of like I was lied to my whole life. The bond is supposed to be this epic connection: like fireworks exploding over the ocean. What the hell does being a virgin have to do with that?

"At least you didn't know the guy. My fated was a close friend."

"Really?" I give him a look. "Why'd she reject you?"

"*He* rejected me." Creed runs his hand through his hair, grinding his jaw.

My mouth forms an O shape, and I search his face. "Your fated was a guy?"

"Yeah. Apparently, he wasn't into the idea of us being together, so he rejected me. It was pretty brutal, because the bond had already started to form but neither of us realized what was going on until I kissed him. You don't really expect same sex fated mates, you know? And he refused to believe he wasn't one-hundred percent straight."

I squeeze his hand. "That must have been hard."

"Yeah," he rasps. "But all things considered, I'm okay."

"How long has it been?"

"Four years," he says, blowing out a hard breath. "And you're the first person I've told about my fated mate being a guy."

"You didn't tell Ronan or Dax?"

He shakes his head. "No. I didn't want it to be weird. I'm

bi, so it was easy enough to pretend like it was a woman who broke my heart."

"If they were real friends, it wouldn't matter to them."

Nodding, he glances away and closes his eyes.

We fall into a comfortable silence, simply holding hands and being there for one another. I'll guard his secret as long as he needs, but I think he should tell Dax and Ronan. I don't think they'd be bothered by it, and he shouldn't have to hide who he is. It doesn't change anything about the time we spent together, and I want to make sure he knows that, so I scoot closer and snuggle into his side, smiling when he wraps his arms around me.

RONAN

The guard arrives about twenty minutes after we shoot the flare off. We covered Seth with a tarp from the supply shed, and sat in silence on the dock, watching the water and wondering if anyone would even come.

"Hey, there." I point to where I see the edge of a boat. There's only one guard, the same one who came out for the last murder. "Took Dean long enough."

"We're the least of his concerns. I'm sure something more important was going on."

"More important than a death?"

Dax scrubs his hair and shoves off the wooden planks, standing and walking to the edge of the dock. "More important than a bunch of rejects nobody wants."

"You sound like Creed," I mutter with a frown.

Creed is always going on about how no one cares about us and they couldn't care less about what happens, and while I've held out hope that we might be able to leave, the stuff with the murders has tarnished my optimism. There are stories of shifters being let off the island and returning to their pack, so that's something. Maybe we can get off the island someday, once we prove we're not feral. Having a mate would help the cause, and I'd be lying if my mind didn't immediately picture Trix.

If she took one of us—or all of us—as a mate, we could ask the High Pack to consider our petition to leave. If it's happened before, it'll happen again.

Unless they're just stories.

Not to mention, Trix may not like any of us, so I shove the thought aside. It was a stupid idea anyway. No one will ever love me. Creed and Dax? Definitely. But me? No way. I may be fun on the surface, but I'm otherwise worthless. My fated rejected me because of it and even my mom told me as much growing up. No one wants a worthless shifter as a mate.

"What took you so long?" Dax asks in a hard voice. His alpha bleeds through when his emotions are high, and Dean glares at him, definitely not appreciating the tone.

Dax may be a reject, but he's still an alpha.

If it weren't for his fancy gun and taser, he'd rip this guy apart.

"We had Wolfe Island business to take care of." Dean whips his sunglasses off and his eyes land on the tarp. "Another body already?"

I clench my mouth shut because nothing I have to say will help anything.

With a nod of understanding to me, Dax takes charge. "He was poisoned, but the killer tried to cover it up by dragging him out to the sonar range."

Dean whistles and sets the glasses on top of his head. "Any leads?"

"No. I thought there was going to be an investigation."

"High Pack business comes first."

"Do you think they'll help us now?" I ask, surging forward.

You'd think I was the hotheaded alpha, but alas, I'm a mere beta with a temper and a healthy distrust of authority.

His hand falls on the butt of his gun. "I'll talk to some people, see if I can get some investigators out."

"That's all we ask," Dax says, stepping in front of me so I can't rush the dude.

"All right. Give me a few days." Dean eyes the tarp again then spins on his heel, strutting back toward his boat.

I start to sputter, but Dax elbows me.

"What about the body?" he asks in a deadly calm voice, which means he's pissed. Dax doesn't get loud when he gets mad, he gets quiet and calculated.

"Bury it somewhere. The High Pack doesn't have resources to deal with this right now." Dean hops onto his boat and pulls the rope from its post. "I'd lock your doors at night if I were you."

The engine sputters to life, and he backs the boat out, staring at us for a few seconds before lowering his sunglasses and taking off toward the main island.

"Are you kidding me?" I shout, not caring who will hear me. "We need help! There's a dead body for fuck's sake."

He holds up his hand in acknowledgement, but doesn't bother turning around.

"Fucking prick," Dax says under his breath.

We turn and look at the tarp at the same time.

"I'll go get the shovels." I storm off, cursing the stupid guard the entire way and hating that Creed had it right.

The High Pack doesn't give a crap about us.

fifteen

BELLATRIX

The guys are gone for a lot longer than we expect, so I keep Creed busy by suggesting we make lunch for them. I don't know if any of us will actually be able to eat given what we witnessed this morning, but at least it keeps our minds occupied. We end up making chicken parmesan, because they had all the necessary ingredients and making a good sauce and fried filet takes time.

We're finishing cooking the chicken when Dax and Ronan crash through the front door covered in dirt. I drop the spatula and rush to them, checking them both over. They're not hurt, but they stink and their shoes and clothes are ruined.

"What happened?" I ask, eyes straying back to Creed.

The poor guy is staring at their shoes, clenching his jaw so tight I'm worried his teeth will crack. "They didn't care, did they?"

I furrow my brow and glance at Dax, hoping he'll clue me in as to what he means.

"No," Dax answers. "Dean said an investigator will come in a few days."

Creed scoffs. "Sure they will."

I look between the men, piecing it together without them needing to say it out loud. They're covered in dirt. No one came to investigate, which means no one took the body.

Shit.

"You had to bury the body."

Dax gives me a sharp nod.

"Fuck." I run my hands through my hair, but my fingers get stuck in the knots Creed put there last night, so it's no use. "Why don't you go clean up. Lunch is almost ready."

"I'm not—"

"Shower. Clean clothes. Get back down here. Understood?" I give Ronan a stern look, daring him to try and argue again.

"Yeah, okay." He ducks his head and leaves the room.

Dax lingers a second, going to Creed and speaking to him in a quiet voice. There's something tender about the way Dax holds his elbow, and I feel like I'm intruding on a private moment. I escape to the bathroom down here to give them a minute, taking advantage of the time and fixing my hair and splashing cool water on my face.

By the time I get back to the kitchen, Creed is the only one there. I meet him at the counter and help spread marinara on the cooked chicken. He puts some parmesan on top, not the fancy kind from the deli, the old school green bottle shaker kind, and he puts the pan in the oven. Since there is limited energy, we set the heat high.

Surprisingly, my stomach grumbles when the timer goes off five minutes later. Creed gives me a little smile and grabs hot pads out of a drawer. The cheese is a glorious blanket of melted goodness on top of the marinara sauce covering the chicken.

"Man, that smells good." Ronan comes in with a towel wrapped around his waist and his hair hanging in loose, wet waves. A few droplets of water skate over his abs and I think I see a hint of a tattoo creeping out of the edge of the towel.

"Oh my god," I say without thinking.

"Trix," Ronan says with a sigh. "I've told you to call me Ronan."

"Shut up." Creed throws a hot pad at his head. "Go put some clothes on, you big bastard."

Ronan flexes, showing off biceps that have to be bigger than my thighs.

"Clothes! Now!" Creed launches another hot pad at him.

"Fine. Don't eat all the food though." Ronan throws the hot pad back at Creed who barely dodges it. "Fucker."

Shaking my head, I raise my eyebrows at Creed once Ronan heads up the stairs.

"You live with him."

He grimaces. "I know."

We share a look, communicating everything without words, because we can't talk about it with the guys in the house. Creed has been surrounded by Mr. Beefcake and the silver fox this entire time while hiding that he's bisexual? He's stronger than I am because I definitely would have tried to make Ronan mine, at least for a few nights, if I were in his place.

"What's with the looks?" Dax asks, entering the kitchen and bringing the soapy scent of fresh rain with him. He's wearing a black t-shirt and jeans, and the scruff covering his jaw should look sloppy, but something about three-day-old beard growth is so perfect on him.

"Nothing," I chirp, grabbing plates from the cabinet and setting them on the counter.

Creed grabs the pasta from the strainer and portions it out. The food isn't gourmet, but it'll be delicious. Besides, a little bit of that green shaker parmesan on top will fix it right up.

Who needs fancy shaved cheese?

After lunch, Dax and Ronan clean the kitchen while Creed and I watch from the barstools. When they finish, we all stare at each other, not quite sure what to say to lighten the mood. Murder is a pretty heavy topic, and we'll have to address it eventually, but for now, I think these guys need to loosen up.

"Do you have alcohol?"

"If you looked in the fridge while you were cooking, you know we do." Dax gives me the side-eye. "Why?"

"What else are we going to do?" I give him a smile, which in all honesty is probably more salty than sweet, and bat my eyelashes.

"Don't make that face," he says, narrowing his gaze. "I forgot how manipulative women could be."

"I'm not manipulative, just using what I was born with."

"Manipulative tendencies?" He smirks.

"Good looks and a pretty smile." I wink at him and hop off the barstool. "Come on, let's drink a little?"

He shoots his gaze over my head, checking in with Creed. "Someone has to stay sober. There's still a killer out there."

"Solid point." I wrinkle my nose. "Maybe a beer each?"

Sighing, he nods and juts his chin toward the fridge. "One apiece."

"Deal," I blurt before he can finish the last word.

Ronan meets me at the fridge, grabbing the door before I can and swinging it open. He hands me a beer, some average domestic kind, and tosses Creed and Dax theirs before grabbing his own. I crack mine, humming in appreciation when the cool lager hits my tongue.

It's no craft beer, but it still hits the spot.

Dax sips his, watching me as I head over to sit next to Creed again. His eyes are knowing, but I'm not embarrassed by what happened between us. I had a lot of fun, and so did Creed. I don't know Dax well enough, but I think I see a tiny flash of envy in his gaze when Creed grins at me and we bump our cans together like we actually have something to celebrate.

"You guys aren't worried about the shops?"

"They'll be okay for a little while," Ronan says, rubbing his lips against the rim of the can. "Mostly people keep to themselves. George was really the one we had to worry about taking more than his fair share... but now he's dead."

And just like that the mood is dreary again.

"What are the others like?" I ask to distract them. "As weird as Dax and Creep here?"

Creed scoffs and gives me a slow once-over. "You didn't think I was weird last night."

Biting my lip, I wink at him. "You were pretty all right."

"Is that why you screamed my name?"

"You're ridiculous." I laugh and take a drink, checking to see how the other two are taking the news.

Ronan tips his head to the side, lost in thought, but Dax is staring at me with less than subtle desire flaring across his features.

"The other guys here are introverted and pretty much avoid us unless they have to come to the shops. Harlow is, well, a handful." Creed shakes his head.

"Tell me more about that." I rest my elbow on the counter and drop my chin on my hand, studying Dax while he processes my sleeping with Creed.

I don't think he's mad about it. I'm pretty sure he's trying to figure out how he can accomplish the same thing, and I'm definitely not opposed to a little silver fox loving. I ignore the little voice in my head that tells me I can't fuck my emotions away because that voice is clearly deluded. Good sex can fix just about anything.

"Harlow punched Ronan."

I swing my gaze to the burly man, eyes widening in disbelief. "How'd she get one in on you?"

"She's fast," he says, shrugging his shoulders. "And she was pissed because I wouldn't let her take an extra box of earl grey tea."

"She didn't want to follow the rules." Dax comes to my other side, scooting the barstool a little closer before sitting down. Our thighs brush, and I pointedly ignore the flutter in my lower stomach.

"It's the principle of the matter." Ronan rolls his head back, trying to work the tension from his neck. "No one else gets to take extra, so why should she?"

"So, no one else drinks tea but her?"

Creed nods. "She's the only one."

Maybe that's what's wrong with her. Too much snobby leaf water makes her grumpy.

"Tell me why you're rationing tea when it clearly doesn't matter to anyone else?"

Ronan shoots his gaze to Dax, who sighs and takes another sip of his beer.

"Because, there are rules."

So strict, he is.

"Do they have to be so rigid?" I turn slightly so I can watch his reaction when I drop my hand onto his thigh.

His nostrils flare a little, and his muscles tense under my fingers, but he doesn't push me away.

Called it. Silver Fox wants some.

"For the sake of peace, I think it's best to stick to the plan. Otherwise people will get mad when we won't let them take more than their share."

I move my hand slightly up his leg, watching as his eyes drop to my hand, and he clenches his teeth together.

"Sometimes it's fun to break the rules."

Creed laughs into his beer, and I picture him shaking his head at me, but I refuse to look away from Dax because he slowly lifts his hooded gaze to meet mine, and what I see there calls to my inner promiscuous bitch. Moons, do I love her.

He puts his hand on top of mine, stopping it before I can get too far and gives me a stern, fatherly look. I'm sure he means to deter me, but if anything, it makes me all the more determined.

"I should go make sure the shops are okay." He lifts my hand, holding on to it as he stands, gripping my fingers for a smidge longer than necessary. "Be nice to my friends."

"Creep and I are tight now. I think I still have to win Ronan over, but something tells me once I kick his ass at poker he'll be a goner too."

"That easy, huh?" Dax says, standing over me.

I tip my head back and chuckle. "They're always easy."

His husky laugh makes my spine tingle, and he lowers his face, stopping mere inches from me. "I like to be chased."

"Is that a request?"

"It's a fact."

"Okay, Old Man. I hear you."

His lips brush over my cheek when he moves to whisper in my ear. "I'm fast, baby girl. Can you keep up?"

Oh. My. Rejected. Mates. Who the hell let this man go? His game is on fire.

"Don't worry about me," I say, fisting his shirt in my hands. "I'm a grown woman."

"I'm counting on it," he says, then draws back, eyes skating to Creed who is sitting quietly behind me.

I don't look away from Dax, but I can feel Creed and Ronan staring at me. When he looks at me again, Dax grips my chin between his thumb and forefinger. My body flushes under their collective attention, and all kinds of scenarios of the three of us together flash through my mind.

"I hope you know what you're doing," he says before stepping away and leaving me with a strange sense of loss.

"Me too," I mutter, turning back to my beer while he leaves.

Ronan comes to the counter, putting his hands on the bar and leaning forward, pinning me with a serious look.

"I'm good at poker."

"I've only played a little," I lie. "Go easy on me?"

He tsks and shakes his head. "You wanted the pain, and I do hate to disappoint. Get your ass in the chair." He points to the desks behind us, and with a demand like that, how can I not comply?

Anything to keep their minds off the murder for a little while longer.

sixteen

BELLATRIX

"What the fuck?" Ronan asks for the third time as I happily set my cards down, showing him my royal flush.

"Sorry, Ronan. Guess it's beginner's luck."

We're sitting around his desk, Ronan on his side and Creed and me across from him. Creed is terrible at poker, but Beefcake is actually pretty good.

Ronan growls softly. "How long have you played?"

I grin. "My dad taught us when we were ten, and we played twice a month."

"Should have known better than to trust a pretty face."

"Oh stop." I pull the cards toward me to start shuffling. "I'm kidding, you can continue."

"I can't believe you got rejected."

Wow, he goes straight for the jugular.

"Yeah, well, I did." This better not turn into one of those *you're so pretty, why are you still single* type of conversations. I will go to the kitchen, channel my inner Harlow and pick out the biggest pan, and smack him in the face if he even thinks about going there.

"Apparently, my fated loved the wolf she'd been dating too much to break up with him for me. He was an alpha, and what good is a beta fated mate to an alpha mate? I kind of respect her for staying true to her boyfriend, but I'm still mad, you know?"

He says all of this like he's talking about some simple slight. The way he glances to the side tells me there's more to the story, or at least more emotion he's not willing to share, so I decide to change the subject. We're supposed to be having fun, not getting depressed.

"Can't say I blame her after seeing your poker skills." I bite my cheek, watching the frown transform into a big grin as he barks out a belly-deep laugh.

Keep them laughing to keep them happy. I think Einstein said that.

Kidding. Obviously, it was George Washington.

"You're funny, Trixie."

I narrow my eyes at the nickname. "Thanks, Ronnie."

He grimaces. "Yeah, okay. Trix it is."

"Thanks, *Ronan*."

Creed covers his mouth with his hand, fighting off a laugh. He's been more than happy watching us trash talk one another and sipping his beer. For a shifter, he's not as possessive as I expected him to be, but I kind of love it. If he doesn't mind me flirting with Ronan, how would he feel about more than flirting? We've only hooked up once, and I'm not exactly in a hurry to get tied down to one man. If I play my cards right, I could potentially have three new playmates, and damn could we have a lot of fun together.

I can feel seriousness creeping in, dampening the mood the more the minutes tick by. I knew there was only so much interference I could run before they circled back to the murders, so I sigh and stack the cards up in a neat pile.

"Okay. Let's make a plan."

They share a look, and I tap the table with my finger.

"Don't think you're excluding me from this."

Creed searches my face. "If you're in, you're all in."

I think he's speaking about more than the murder, but I

decided earlier when he tried to save that shifter I wasn't
going to go back to my house. I'm safer here, and I like them.
Sex absolutely has nothing to do with it. Not one bit.

"I'm in."

DAX

About two hours into my shift, Trix wanders up the road.
She's searching the trees, trying to spot the guard tower, but
she won't find it. We made sure to make it discrete when we
built it. Sticking my fingers in my mouth, I whistle. Her head
whips in my direction, and a smirk crawls across her face.
She lifts two cans of beer in salute and heads over. I groan
and scrub my hand over my face.

She's the worst sort of distraction, but I'll be damned if I
tell the little vixen to leave. It's rare you meet a woman so
confident in herself and her desires, and seeing as I'm stuck
on this fucking island for the rest of my extended life, I'm
going to enjoy her company.

When she reaches the tree, I move to watch her climb the
ladder. From here I can see straight down her shirt, and if I
were a stronger man, I'd look away out of respect.

I'm weak as fuck.

"These steps look rotten," she mutters, slipping a beer in
the front of her shorts and the other under her chin.

"You'll be all right. Are my friends all in one piece?"

As soon as she gets to the top, she sets a beer on the platform. Her bright eyes flash to mine, mirth dancing in her
gaze. "For now."

I grin and look away, drawing my top teeth over my
bottom lip. She has no right to be so funny. She climbs all the
way up, grabs the beer can from her shorts, and sits in one of
the folding chairs and kicks her foot up on the railing.

"So you still maintaining that *I'm not a stalker* bit?"

"I'm not."

She snorts. "You sit up here and watch people all day."

"It's different."

"You stood outside of my house and stared into my windows."

"Well that's definitely different."

"How?" she demands, gesturing to the beer she brought for me.

I bend and scoop it up, side-eyeing her as I do. "Because that would make me a peeping tom, not a stalker."

"Now you're talking semantics."

"Maybe," I say with a laugh. "What are you doing out here?"

She sighs. "They're planning the murderer's demise, and I've run out of ideas. I don't know anyone, so I'm no help brainstorming who it could be."

I should be there with them, but the guys will fill me in later. Aside from wanting to spend some more time with Trix, I feel obligated to keep an eye on things. My alpha nature drives me to be in charge, to take some sort of control where there is no authority. Letting things be would have never worked out. It was either me taking charge, or me fighting whoever tried to do it for the spot. The only other alpha that was on the island was George, but he was too messed up in the head because of his rejection to try and challenge me.

"What's your favorite movie?" I push the chair next to her a little closer before sitting down and putting my arm on the back of hers. She barely reacts, but I see her lips quirk.

"Fight Club."

"The one with the rule?" I ask, surprised she'd be into that type of movie. I've only seen it once, but it was pretty insane.

"There are actually eight."

"Pardon me. The one with eight rules is your favorite?"

She looks down at the shops and nods. "My dad really liked it."

Sensing her desire to change topics, I say, "I like Lord of the Rings."

"Hmm. But do you partake in elevenses?"

"From time to time." I pop the tab of my beer and take a swig, deciding I'm still sober enough for another one. Since we don't drink often, and we ration how much we have, one beer is almost enough to get me buzzed, but it's been about two hours since I drank the other one.

"Dream car?" she asks, leaning all the way back in her seat.

Running a finger over her shoulder, I consider the question. It's been so long since I thought about luxury items. "I really like the old broncos."

"I think I'd want a McLaren."

"Can you even drive standard?"

She snorts. "Trust me, I know my way around a stick."

"Oh yeah?"

"Mmhmm. Hiking or swimming?"

"Hiking," I say immediately. After seeing a man drown, swimming is at the bottom of my list.

"Same." She shoots me a grin and sighs. "So this is what you do all day? Don't you get bored?"

"Of course, but we've learned to make the most of it. We could be miserable fucks who mope around all day."

Putting her beer down, she turns in her seat, hooking her ankle under her other leg.

"What's your story?" she asks. "I'll tell you mine."

"Nothing unique. I met my fated two years ago, but I was already old and she'd just turned eighteen."

"Oh. Age gap. Love it." She thinks for a minute then

cringes. "Sorry, obviously I don't love it if she rejected you. She's a cunt."

I scoff. "She was nice. I rejected her."

Trix takes in a sharp breath. "You did what?"

Running my hand over my beard, I nod. "Yeah. She was so young. She had a boyfriend, and then we crossed paths and bam, her whole life would have been wasted on an old man. I would have died before her, only causing her more pain as the bond would have been fully set. I couldn't bring myself to put her through that."

"Wow." She pinches her eyebrows together. "Do you know how much it hurts to be rejected?"

The question isn't meant to be rude. She's curious, and I don't think she's judging me for what I did. I feel remorse for the little bit of pain I caused her, but with my rejection and volunteering to leave, she got to stay. The circumstances were unique enough my alpha agreed to it. Most times it's the rejected that gets shipped off, but even he knew it should be me who got shipped away for life and not her.

"It hurt me to do it, so I imagine it's similar, but probably worse for the person being rejected."

"My fated and I met for all of one minute before he rejected me, and it felt like someone had taken a piece of my soul. I tried to do it first, but he was an alpha and his rejection trumped mine."

"Why'd he reject you?" I ask, wondering if she'll clam up and shut me out for prying, but she doesn't. I take a drink to give her time to respond.

"Apparently, being a virgin was a prerequisite, and I didn't get the memo."

I choke. "Fuck." Pounding my fist on my chest to get rid of the burning sensation, I cough. "You're kidding, right?"

What is it with some shifter packs worshiping virgins?

I've never understood it. Of course, a bond where you're both each other's first is probably fucking amazing, but there's nothing wrong with experience. At my age, I definitely prefer it and that's part of why I rejected my fated too. It didn't feel right being that much older than her and possibly taking her virginity all the while knowing I was going to be the reason her heart broke and soul shattered when I died.

"I wish," she mutters. "So, here I am. The whore of Pack Ozark."

The laugh she releases is humorless and her eyes darken with self-loathing, but she shakes it off a second later and grins.

"His name was Chad."

"Oh wow. Definitely not worth it then."

She snorts, then slaps her hand over her mouth.

"Oink-oink." I pinch her neck, lightly tugging on her skin.

"Shut up." She elbows me and rolls her eyes. "So yeah, now you know my story. And you're wrong, by the way."

"What?" I ask, entirely not following her train of thought.

"Her life wouldn't have been wasted."

The sincerity in her gaze is too much for me to handle. I swallow the sudden lump in my throat and glance away, eyeing the grocery store.

"Hungry?"

"It's a constant state of being for me." Her mouth pulls into a grave line, and her eyes grow serious.

I shake my head and bite back a grin. "Come on, Trix. Let's go break some rules."

Her eyes widen, and she jumps out of her seat, clapping her hands and shaking her hips. "I knew you'd cave, Old Man."

Grunting at the nickname, I slam my beer and toss it into the trash can.

Trix sighs in a rather dramatic way and puts her hand on her chest. "Grumpy and responsible."

"You're a brat, you know that?"

"Absolutely." Her shit eating grin draws a ridiculous smile from me, and she winks at me. "Time to break some rules."

seventeen

RONAN

We don't get much further in our scheming after Trix leaves. Neither of us are investigators, and Creed is half listening. His eyes keep straying to the window, his attention obviously drifting to a pretty blonde with a great rack. Can't say I blame him. Trix is funny, gorgeous, and is easy to talk to.

"So, what's happening with you and Trix?"

He shrugs. "I don't know. We slept together, and I like her."

"You think that's a good idea?" I'm not trying to discourage him. I'm genuinely curious. She was flirting with me, and he didn't mind one bit. If he's ready to pursue a relationship, I don't want to fuck it up for him.

"I think we could all use a little feminine attention."

Shuffling the cards a few times, I watch the laminated paper fan apart and weave together. "What about Dax?"

"We've been living together for two years, sharing things the entire time. I think we'll figure it out."

He's so matter of fact about it, which is probably a good thing. Still though, we may all be more than happy to share, but we don't know that she will be. By nature, Trix is fun and flirtatious. That doesn't mean she'll want me. I can tell she's attracted to Dax, and while she and I made easy banter during our poker game, it was hard to tell what she thought of me.

I won't stand in their way if they want to pursue her, but I'll have to take some steps to protect myself from another rejection. It won't be nearly as hurtful as the fated mate bond breaking, but I can only be told I'm worthless and unwanted so many times.

Trix will be good for my friends though, and even if she and I are never more than friends, it'll be refreshing to have another person around.

~

BELLATRIX

Walking through the small store with Dax is oddly familiar, almost like we've done it a hundred times before. Probably because we get along so well. My eyes catch on a bright red package and I grab his arm, stopping him.

"I love Munchos."

"You already picked out candy, cookies, and beef jerky."

Narrowing my eyes, I give him a pointed look, silently reminding him that this was his idea and he can't be a party pooper.

"Fine. Get them."

"Thank you." I snatch the bag up and glance around the shelves once more, eye the small basket Dax is carrying, and decide I really have gotten enough food.

"Oh, so now we're letting people take whatever they want?" an incredibly pissed off voice asks from behind us.

We both spin around in surprise, and I take in Harlow's haggard appearance. I've only really seen her once, but something tells me the pajama look she's rocking is not her usual style.

"Right. You like tea," I say, moving down the aisle to where the boxes are. "What's your favorite?"

She scowls at me, then glares at Dax. "The spicy chai."

"Really, Dax? There are at least twenty boxes here." I shake my head at his ridiculous rule and gesture Harlow over. "Bring me your basket."

Eyeing me like I'm not trustworthy, she slowly steps around Dax and comes to stand by me. I take her basket and put it next to the shelf, then use my arm to sweep every last box into it, assuming she used all her loose leaf chai and needs the backup.

"Trix," Dax groans, but I shush him and grin at Harlow. "Stupid ass rules, am I right?"

Her face softens a little, and I see a hint of a smile. "Pretty much."

"Need anything else?"

Waving me off, she grabs her basket. "I can get it." She flips Dax off. "I think Bellatrix should be in charge."

"Call me Trix."

She looks at me, still a little guarded, but nods. "Trix for president."

Bursting into an obnoxious laugh, I pump my fist into the air. "Let chaos reign!"

"You're insane," Harlow whispers. "But I think I like it. Sorry for the pan."

I shrug. "I'd do the same. Don't let Dax push you around though. If he gives you a hard time, you tell me."

"Trix, you're going to get spanked if you keep it up."

His words only make me grin. Harlow volleys her gaze between us.

"What's it like having a magical vagina?"

"I haven't slept with him yet."

She lifts an eyebrow. "Yet. See? Magical vagina. Bitch."

"If it makes you feel better, this magical vagina also got rejected."

Frowning at that, she sighs. "It shouldn't, but it does."

"Are you okay?" I ask, following her as she picks out a few other things.

"As okay as I can be," she confesses. "Being exiled is one thing, but worrying about getting killed sucks."

"Yeah. Do you want to stay with me and the guys? You shouldn't be all alone."

She stiffens and her smile falls. "I'm fine. I don't need your help."

Confused by her sudden shift in mood, I ease away from her. "Okay. The offer still stands though."

"Thanks, but no thanks." She grabs a bag of Fritos and turns to Dax. "When does the next shipment drop?"

"Next week."

"Can you ask them if they're going to bring more eggs? It's been two shipments without some."

My eyes slide to the shelf, where only one carton sits. Now I understand why Dax is so strict about rationing. Harlow isn't pushing to take the last of them, but she sounds genuinely concerned.

"Yeah. I reminded them, but you know how they are."

Harlow scoffs. "Yeah, I do." Then she walks out of the store without saying goodbye and taking the basket with her.

"She'll bring it back later," Dax says, gaze following her retreating back.

"Is she always so defensive?" I whisper, hoping she's far enough away to miss the question.

He puts his finger to his lips and tips his head toward the door. I sigh and nod, following him out. Only when we get back to the guard tower and Harlow is completely out of sight does he answer.

"She used to work for the guard."

"Oh wow." Did not see that coming.

"Yeah, so when she catches herself getting a little too chatty with us rejects, she slips into her old habits, forgetting that she's also a reject. I don't think she realizes how rude she can be; it's ingrained in her to put distance between herself and us."

"Old habits die hard, I guess."

"Hmm." He sits and I take my seat, gazing around the island from the perch. Wolfsbane is beautiful, and it would have been the type of place I'd want to vacation if I were still free to do so.

I frown for what feels like the millionth time in a week and sigh. I don't know if I'll ever get used to being stuck, but I have to try.

A FEW DAYS LATER I WAKE UP IN CREED'S BED ALONE AND naked. There's no sense in wearing clothes to bed with him. I stretch, spreading myself across his mattress and loving how good I feel. He has not disappointed in bed, and to be honest, I'm a little disappointed he isn't here now because I woke up horny. Rolling on my side, I tuck my arm under my pillow and listen for any sign of life in the house.

No one is home.

That's a bit strange, but they do have their own lives to live. I've already gotten used to being around at least one of them at all times. Being alone isn't necessarily a bad thing, but being alone inside their house is new for me.

The ache between my legs isn't going away, and it doesn't help that I'm in Creed's room, breathing in his masculine, woodsy scent and smelling the evidence of what we did last night. The sweet smell lingers, taunting me with what I can't have.

My core tightens when an after pang—you know, the phantom thrust a day after sex that makes you clench in need for that same person?—hits me. I bury my nose in his pillow and groan. This is unacceptable.

With a frustrated huff, I roll onto my back and decide I'm perfectly capable of taking care of things myself. I may not have any toys, but I have practiced fingers. I glide my palm down my stomach, slipping a finger through my folds. Using the other hand, I pinch my nipple and tug on it, working myself in the best way I know how.

The thing about masturbation? Everything has to be a little bit harder, a little more intense, to get a reaction. Whereas with a man, it's a little easier. There's something so erotic about the heat of another body pressing against mine, like I'm taking a bit of that warmth for myself.

I bite my lip, moving my finger faster over my clit, chasing an orgasm. A large thud sounds from downstairs, making me squeal. I forget all about making myself come and roll off the bed, landing in a crouch.

Fuck. I'm naked.

Quickly tugging on my shorts and Creed's shirt, I hold my breath, waiting to see if I hear another thud. All I hear is the steady rhythm of a heartbeat coming from downstairs. Maybe it's one of the guys?

A full minute passes without another loud sound. Frowning, I walk out of the room and stop at the top of the stairs.

"Hello?"

No answer.

My pulse pounds, and I stay completely still, wondering if this is how I die. The murderer is still on the loose, and I don't smell or hear any of the guys. After staying with them for a few days, I know their breathing, their scents, and the way they walk.

You don't know them that well.

Though my inner voice may be a bitch, she's right. Perhaps I'm not as in tune with the guys as I thought.

I shake my head at how scared I was for a few seconds, and take the first step down. Feet shuffle across the floor downstairs, light and not at all how I'd expect the guys to move. I freeze, wrapping my fingers around the railing. My enhanced hearing picks up a heartbeat and faint breathing, like the person is trying not to be noticed.

Why would they sneak around their own house?

That doesn't make sense.

My mind races with the worst-case scenarios, and my chest tightens as anxiety swirls in my stomach.

"Who's there?" I ask, thudding down a few steps louder than necessary in an attempt to scare them off.

It must work, because the back door bangs open, I run down the stairs and race out of the house. I stumble to a stop on the small back porch, glancing from side to side. Sniffing softly, I wrinkle my nose when I'm greeted with an unusual smell. The intruder, because I've surmised none of my guys were here, is a man. His scent is barely discernible over the reek of gasoline. The smell is so strong it's almost like he doused himself in fuel to cover his tracks.

Stomping feet race through the house. A sigh of relief rushes out of me and my shoulders sag. They're back.

"Trix!" Dax roars, though his voice is more desperate than angry.

"I'm here!" I call, wrapping my arms around my middle.

Searching the trees once more, I frown at the thought of someone coming into the house with the men gone. Had the person known I was left alone? I turn around in time to see Creed and Dax burst through the door. Dax's eyes are glowing yellow and a growl rumbles in Creed's chest.

"Someone was here," I say, gesturing in the direction I think he went. "He ran into the trees."

Dax gives me a curt nod before stripping and shifting,

taking off into the trees in his wolf form to chase after the intruder.

"Are you okay?" Creed pulls me into a hug, wrapping me in his strong arms.

"Yeah. A little shaken up." I breathe him in, replacing the stench of gasoline with his warmth and comfort. "Do you think that was the killer?"

He shakes his head, chin brushing over the top of my head. "I don't know. Whoever it was will regret coming here."

I don't doubt it. Shifters are possessive by nature, so someone breaking in is a direct threat to what they consider their territory. I chew on my lip and glance behind me. Dax is nowhere in sight, but a howl rises up through the trees, frustrated and angry.

"Shit," Creed mutters. "Let's go inside to wait for him. He'll be at it for a while."

Alphas take challenges very personally, and while the intruder may not have declared a verbal challenge, trespassing is enough to trigger that instinct within Dax.

"Where were you guys?" I don't like how whiny I sound, but it isn't like them to leave me alone without saying something.

He guides me through the door and into the kitchen. "A pipe burst and we had to fix it. Dax needed help welding, so I had to go. I left you a note, but I guess you didn't see it."

"No. A sound woke me up but I hadn't gone downstairs yet when I realized someone was in the house."

I sit at the bar, resting my elbow on the counter and putting my chin in my hands. Creed studies the room, eyes tracing over every inch like he might find some clue as to who broke in.

Wrinkling my nose, I hop up and go open a window. "Whoever he is stinks."

"He wanted to cover his tracks. I shouldn't have left you

alone. Ronan was on his shift, so I thought it would be safe. He's not that far away."

"He probably thought I was making the noise. I wouldn't have considered someone breaking in either." I sigh and head to the fridge. There are no eggs, but we have jelly and bread, so I grab the jar of strawberry and pop two pieces of bread in the toaster.

"You want some?"

Creed shakes his head, running his hands through his blond hair and messing it up. He's rattled, so I try to distract him by asking about the burst pipe. Apparently, the infrastructure here is about ten years old, so while things are relatively new, they'll begin to slowly wear down. We're lucky Dax knows what he's doing, because I doubt many shifters know how to do the work that needs to be done.

Dax storms into the house about the time I finish eating my toast. He prowls to where I sit, putting his arms on either side of me and caging me against the bar. I spin in my seat, leaning back so I can peer up at him. His gaze travels over me before settling on mine.

"Hey, Old Man."

He growls. "Trix."

"Did you find him?" I ask.

"No." A muscle jumps in his stubble covered jaw. The black and gray whiskers are long enough to look soft. I reach up and stroke his beard.

"Are you okay?"

He closes his eyes and leans into my touch, taking a deep breath before nodding. I run my fingers over his beard for a few more seconds then pull away. His hand shoots up to keep my palm against his skin. His grip is firm, but it doesn't hurt. Blue irises pierce through me, and without him needing to say it, I realize he's most upset about me being in danger.

Placing his other hand on my shoulder, he rests his forehead against mine and breathes. I watch a dozen thoughts flash over his face, all of them deepening the lines of his frown.

"I've got a killer left hook," I whisper, hoping for a grin.

"That doesn't mean you're safe," he says. "If he hurt you—"

"He didn't," I say. "I'm happy you care, but don't waste time worrying about what could have been. You're here now and I know you'll protect me. That's all that matters."

"Now you're kissing my ass," he mumbles, but his lips kick up into a proud smile.

"Maybe." I shrug. "But I'm not wrong. With you guys here, he won't come back."

Because the killer wants easy prey.

"You can't be left alone," Creed says from the other side of the counter.

I look over my shoulder at him. "But you can?"

He grimaces. "We can double up the guard shifts at night, that way none of us are left alone when we're most vulnerable?"

"Good idea. I'll go check on Ronan." Dax kisses my palm before leaving, and I stare at my hand for a moment.

For some reason I didn't expect him to be so tender, but I can't say I'm disappointed. It's nice for someone to be so worried about me they need to feel my touch to ground themselves. If being a reject means I get to live with the three of them for the rest of my life, I'm in.

If a murderer could NOT ruin things for me, that'd be great.

eighteen

BELLATRIX

The next afternoon, while Dax is sleeping off his guard shift and Creed is working, Ronan and I relax inside. We had a quiet morning of hanging out together in companionable silence, so when he abruptly stands from his desk and tosses his cards down, I stop reading and eye him.

"What's wrong?" I ask, sticking an old scrap of paper to mark my spot in the historical romance I found on a bookshelf in the living room.

"I'm going for a walk."

"Okay. I'll come with you."

His eyebrows pinch together and he purses his lips.

"Unless you don't want me to?" I try not to sound bothered by his reaction, but the way his face instantly softens tells me I did a bad job of concealing my emotions.

"No, it's okay. You can come with."

"I don't mind staying behind if you'd rather be alone." And now I sort of don't want to go if the thought of me coming really bothers him so much. Glancing back at my book, I start to skim the page I'd been reading, giving him the opportunity to escape without it getting more awkward.

Fuck emotions. I hate them.

"Trix," he says.

"Hmm?" I don't look up.

If I ignore him, he'll leave me alone. Though I'm pretty

sure if he leaves, I'll be more upset than if he stays to try and talk it out with me. See? Emotions are stupid.

Maybe I'm PMSing.

He sighs heavily, and I hear him walk over to where I'm sitting on the couch. Out of my peripheral vision, I see him scratch his beard. I let him sweat, because it would sound really crazy if I blurted out how much his reaction bothered me. Besides, if he wants me to be a part of his life, he'll need to figure out whatever it is he's going through and stop pushing me away.

"Trix." His voice is softer, more insistent, so I glance at him.

"Ronan."

He extends his hand and gives me a hopeful smile. "Walk with me?"

"It's fine, really. I know you probably want to have alone time. You don't have to offer because you feel bad for me."

"I don't feel bad for you."

I lift an eyebrow. "This isn't a pity ask?"

"No. I want you to come with me. I didn't mean to make that face, I just… My head's all fucked up." Ronan looks at his feet and sticks his hands in his pockets.

"Do you want to talk about it?" I ask, setting the book aside and standing. I take a step into his space. "I'm a great listener."

"I like you, Trix."

I grin. "I like you too, Big Guy."

A pained look crosses his face, and he shakes his head, like he doesn't believe me or something. Blowing out a hard breath, he curses.

"I'm such a downer. I'm sorry."

"Wow. Listen to that negative self-talk. Why do you think you're a downer?" I ask, putting my hand on his chest. "The Ronan I know is hilarious."

He searches my face, and I think he might open up. He's on the verge of letting me in and telling me what he's thinking when Creed bangs into the house.

"Babe! I'm so fucking thirsty, and it's not just water I want!"

I can't help but laugh at that, and for some reason my response makes Ronan pull away. I drop my hand, giving him a confused look, but he turns to glance at Creed.

"Water is all you get because you're still on duty."

"I know." Creed groans, grabbing a cup and filling it with tap water. "What are you guys doing?"

"Going for a walk," I say, snatching Ronan's hand before he can protest and dragging him toward the front door. "I'll see you tonight about your thirst. I might be able to help."

Creed chuckles darkly, and I know exactly where his mind went. Mine is more worried about Ronan though, so I continue pulling him out of the house and toward the small dirt path in the trees.

Now maybe he'll talk.

~

RONAN

HER SKIN IS SO SOFT BUT HER GRIP IS STRONG. SHE REFUSES TO let me go when I try to pull my hand back, and part of me is glad she denies me because I'm a masochist and like torturing myself with things I can't have.

"So," she begins, "Do you want to tell me what's going on with you?"

I shake my head. "I'm fine, Trix. How about you? How are you handling everything?"

Perhaps turning the tables on her is a little rude, but it

diverts the attention from me to her. Besides, she hasn't mentioned much of anything about her family and I know she must miss them. I expect her to change the subject because she doesn't like talking about her emotions either, but she surprises me.

"I've been avoiding thinking about it for the most part. I don't know if I'll get used to the idea of never seeing my family again. I miss them so much." She side-eyes me. "What about you? Do you miss your family?"

Grimacing, I look through the trees, ducking under a low branch as we walk. It's pretty warm out today, but the humidity makes it a bit uncomfortable. Sweat breaks out across my forehead because of it, not because of her question.

"I actually miss my friends the most."

She nods, biting her lip and frowning. "Your parents?"

I shrug. "A bit. I miss having a mom, but I don't miss my mom, if that makes sense." Since she's being honest, I may as well be. It's not like the guys and I get deep into our emotions, so this is the first time I've talked about how I feel.

"I'm sorry. Do you want to talk about it?"

"You know how parents are supposed to be this unshake-able pillar of support and unconditional love?"

Her face softens and her eyes drift to the side, a small grin pulls at her lips. "Yeah."

She's probably thinking about her family. From what I've gathered from the little she's said, she had a great childhood. Such a difference from what I experienced growing up. As if realizing this might be the case, her smile falls and her eyes fill with worry.

"My mom was always there, but her love was condi-tional… and she hardly ever showed me her support. I heard how pathetic I was more than how she loved me." I grind my teeth together and stare straight ahead, unable to watch Trix's face fill with pity.

We walk for a few minutes in silence; Trix's fingers tighten around mine, like she's trying to comfort me without being overly obvious. She stops, and I turn to face her, swallowing the lump in my throat when I see nothing but affection in her eyes.

"You're not pathetic, Ronan."

I wrinkle my forehead. "How do you know that?"

Scoffing, she drops my hand and pokes my chest. "Because I've seen you take care of Dax and Creed. I've seen how you look after the house. How you care about whether they're too tired for their shifts. You're not pathetic at all, Ronan. You're amazing."

"Trix, you don't have to try to make me feel better."

She narrows her eyes. "I'm not trying to make you feel anything. I'm stating facts. You know what's pathetic? A mom telling her son he's pathetic. That's disgusting. She's supposed to love you, not treat you like shit. You didn't deserve that. Hell, no kid deserves that sort of parenting."

"Sometimes I wish there were at least one thing wrong with you," I mutter, running my hands over my face.

Laughing a little, she pinches her eyebrows together. "I definitely fart. Does that make you feel better?"

"Oh that's disgusting, Trix." I pretend to be offended. "Thanks for telling me before I fall too hard."

She shoves my chest again, giggling and grabbing my hand so we can continue our walk. I bite my cheek, shooting a quick glance in her direction. She's smiling, and for some reason seeing her happy makes me happy.

That's when I know I'm in danger.

I know there's this stigma that big guys are supposed to be macho, manly men who don't acknowledge their feelings, but I'll be the first to admit, at least to myself, that I have a lot of emotions and they're loud. Like all the love I was denied growing up made me desperate for connection, and now that Trix has shown me an ounce of kindness, I want to wrap her up in my arms and keep her to myself.

Only she's not mine, and she probably never will be.

I have to be careful, because she makes it easy to forget about keeping my distance. I have to protect myself from getting hurt again.

CREED

I'm sitting in the guard tower for my night shift, hating that I have to stay awake for another six hours and Trix isn't with me. She's at home with Ronan and Dax, but Dax will be here soon enough to keep me company. While I think I'd be okay by myself, she insisted we stick to the double guard at night. It's cute she's worried about us, but the arrangement is cutting into my time with her.

The street lamp a few feet over lights the area around me, and I watch as Dax walks down the road, heading for the tower.

"Hey, man."

"Hey," I call.

He climbs up the ladder, taking the extra chair next to me. He sets his hands behind his head and sticks his feet out, taking up as much space as he can.

Such an alpha move.

I try not to stare at the strip of abs I can see, but my gaze strays that direction before I can stop it.

"Jealous?" Dax asks, running his palm over his stomach.

Swallowing down the flare of lust rising within me, I pull my eyes from his abs and meet his, shaking my head. "No way. Mine are better."

He lifts an eyebrow. "Yeah right. Show me." There's a glint of a challenge in his irises, like he doesn't think I'll do it.

Standing, I yank my shirt up and slip my thumb in my shorts, pulling them down a little so he can see almost the entire V. That's the important part. The street lamp doesn't offer much light, but I swear his pupils dilate when he traces his eyes down my stomach.

Sometimes I'm not sure what to think about him. There are days where I'm pretty certain he's flirting with me, but before I can figure out if he is, he backs all the way off and I wonder if I imagined the whole thing in my head. I always wrote it off as my imagination running wild since it had been so long since I'd gotten laid, but now that I've been having plenty of sex, I know I'm not imagining the way his eyes grow hooded or the way his tongue darts out to wet his lips.

Brushing my thumb over my skin, I put my shorts back in the right place and pull my shirt down, watching him tuck away his reaction before he meets my gaze. It's too late though, because I watched him the entire time, and I know he liked what he saw.

A beat of silence passes, and I start to worry he's going to react the same way my best friend did when he realized we were fated mates.

"Don't worry, bro. We can both be hot," I say, running my hand through my hair and sitting back down.

"I'm definitely hotter," he jokes, slapping my arm with his hand.

"At least you're humble about it," I mumble.

He laughs. "Anything interesting happen before I got here?"

I release a soft breath, relieved that the moment didn't ruin everything between us. I'm attracted to Dax, but I don't want to fuck up our friendship by admitting as much to him.

Best to pretend like nothing happened, right?

nineteen

BELLATRIX

An entire week passes without incident. I accompany each of the men on a night shift, insisting that I pull my weight because it's not fair for them to be working so hard when I can help too. Plus, it gives me time to spend with each of them. Ronan is still a little guarded, but day by day he softens. Whatever is going on inside of his head is a mystery, but I make sure he feels included when I'm around him and the other guys.

I think he's threatened by me. Like maybe he thinks I'll replace him as part of the trio, but that would never happen because it's more than clear Creed and Dax love him like a brother. I start to see how my future will play out the more I spend time with them. Creed and I have been sharing a bed, but he isn't bothered when Ronan or Dax flirt with me. If anything, he eggs them on. I'm definitely not complaining, because I like all three of them. They're not my family, but they're quickly becoming close friends… and maybe even lovers. One can dream, at least.

Not bothering to brush my sex-head hair, I stumble down the stairs to start the coffee. My core throbs with delicious reminders of what Creed did to my body last night, and I'm so distracted rubbing my eyes I don't see Ronan until I crash into him.

His hands grab my waist to keep me upright, and he takes a long deep inhale, groaning in frustration.

"I'm going to kill him."

"You can't do that. I think I love his penis."

Ronan chuckles darkly, pulling me closer. "I can fix that."

This is my favorite side of Ronan. When I catch him so off guard he forgets to pretend like he doesn't want me. Maybe it's because I reek of sex, or because I'm only wearing a t-shirt that he's decided to pull me closer rather than push me away.

Giving him a hard glare, I shake my head. "You can't kill Creed. I asked for it."

And, man, did he deliver.

The coffee machine whirs in the background, and as soon as it starts to drip the bitter aroma floats in the air. I'm so exhausted I don't care that Ronan is still holding me, nor do I care when he drops his nose to my neck, inhaling again.

He groans then pulls back to look at me. "He's an asshole."

"You're torturing yourself," I say, wrapping my arms around his neck. "Feeling neglected?"

Walking me toward the counter, he picks me up and sets me on the ledge, pushing between my legs.

"What if I am?"

Man, he's feisty this morning. Rather than pointing that out, I tip my head to the side and shrug. "Well, I can think of a few ways to—"

Dax bursts into the house, eyes landing on us and widening. "Forget the coffee, we have a new shifter."

His words snap Ronan out of his lust-induced haze, and he steps out of my reach. "Already?"

I want to cry at the loss of his nearness, but that's crazy talk. I don't chase men unless they ask me to, especially not ones who can't decide if they want me or if they would rather keep their distance. There will be no running after Ronan. I eye his long hair, which is artfully tied in a man bun.

Fuck. Maybe I'll power walk after him. Definitely no running though.

"Yeah, we should go help him."

Wait a minute. "Why didn't the greeting committee come for me?"

Neither of them answer, and I huff, assuming the worst. "Well, that's sexist. You'll help the man but not me?"

"Can we talk about it later?" Ronan pleads, grabbing a few disposable Styrofoam cups and lining them up by the coffee pot.

"Fine," I say, tucking my hair behind my ear. "But there better be a good reason."

Creed comes down the stairs, giving me a lazy, cocky smile when he sees my hair.

"A good reason for what?"

"Why didn't I get a welcoming committee but this new bloke gets one."

He pauses, eyes flitting to the other two, who give nothing away. "There's a new guy?" he asks instead of answering my question.

Dax nods. "Come on."

"Here," Ronan shoves a coffee into my hand. I guzzle it down, ignoring the burn, and quickly finger comb my hair. It's not perfect, but I get the biggest knots out.

CREED

I'm surprised they didn't rat me out, seeing as I'm the one who left her to fend for herself, but happy they didn't because it'll give me time to figure out how to tell her that I saw her get tased and then left her. A total dick move, but hopefully she'll understand.

We run to the dock, arriving as the boat full of guards

leaves. A man is face down on the grass, groaning as he pushes to all fours.

Trix gasps then growls. All three of us look at her, but her gaze is set on the newcomer and rage is flaring in her eyes. I look at the guy again, this time with suspicion.

There's really only one reason she'd be so pissed.

But there's no way her fated would end up here too, right?

"What the fuck are *you* doing here?" she seethes, prowling toward him and curling her fingers into fists at her side.

Shit. It is her fated.

Dax is the first to snap out of the surprise, grabbing her around the waist and pulling her against his body. She jerks, but he locks his arms around her to keep her in place. The guy finally stops groaning and gets to his knees, staring at Trix like he has the right to do so.

"Don't look at her," I snap, rushing toward him.

His gaze swings to mine, tension drawing his shoulders up. "Like you can stop me."

Dax and Ronan both growl in response, clearly in agreement with this guy needing to get his ass kicked.

"Of course you already fucked someone else." The guy sneers at Trix. "Guess I was right. You *are* despicable. Who'd want you as their fated?"

I surge forward, but Dax releases Trix, and she beats me to the guy, cracking her palm across his cheek hard enough to whip his head to the side. Pride swells in my chest as I watch her. She's so fucking perfect.

"You're an asshole." She shoves his chest, and his eyes flash yellow as he almost loses control of his wolf. "You're the one who isn't worthy."

His face contorts with anger, and he slowly rises, towering over her. Dax, Ronan, and I close the distance and fan out behind her, letting this guy know if he has a problem with our little bundle of chaos, he'll have to deal with the three of us.

"Enjoy the slut." He hisses the last word before taking off into the trees.

"I'm going to kick his ass," Dax mutters, starting after him, but Trix whirls and grabs his arm.

"Don't. He's not worth your time."

"What the hell is he doing here?" Ronan asks even though he knows we don't have any more information than he does.

"He must have snapped," I say, eyeing Trix. Usually the rejectors get to stay with their pack, unless they start to show signs of going feral. A rejector being affected by the bond breaking is rare, but it has been known to happen. "You're not a slut."

She smiles at me. "Thanks." Controlling her emotions as best she can, she sighs and turns away, but not before I see the slight misting of tears in her eyes.

She's tough, but being close to the fated mate who rejected you then hurled insults at you has to be hard. This guy brings nothing but pain for her. And it shouldn't make me so angry, but right now I'm forcing myself to stay put rather than hunting the douche down and introducing him to my fist.

Oh shit.

I'm in trouble because I like her. A lot.

twenty

RONAN

Trix and I are sitting in the guard tower the next time Chad makes himself known. He shows up around three in the afternoon, waltzing down the street like he's hot shit. Trix seethes in her seat, shooting daggers at him.

"I'll get rid of him," I say, already out of my seat and heading toward the ladder. Ever since the incident a few days ago, I've been waiting for a moment to rip into him. The things he said to her still roll around in my head, making me angry every time I think about them.

"I'll go with you."

"You don't have to," I say, stopping on the first step down and meeting her fiery gaze. "I don't want him near you."

The further away she is, the more I can protect her from his douchery.

She smiles at that, but stands. "He's an alpha, and if he wants to start shit, someone needs to be there to have your back."

Solid point. I'm only a beta, and no matter how much muscle I have on him, he'll be stronger and faster. Worst case scenario, she can run and get Dax.

"Stay behind me." I continue down the ladder.

With a soft chuckle, she begins her descent. "It's cute you think I'll listen to you."

If it weren't for the bastard on the ground, I'd take this moment to show her exactly how much she'd listen to me if I really wanted her to. Something about her fated's arrival makes me feel like proving myself to her, like I can make her happy even though I know she deserves better than me. It doesn't make any sense to want her this much when it'll never work out.

I wait for her to get down before heading out of the trees, cutting Chad off.

Trix links her arm through mine and leans into my side, surprising me and him.

"Settling in, dickwad?" Her tone is sugary sweet, but the words are sharp like a knife.

"Fuck you, cunt."

I swear this motherfucker is going down.

"Listen, Chad. You have three seconds to tell me what the fuck you want before shit starts to get real." I pull out of Trix's hold and press into his space. "Seeing as I've been here for a lot longer, I have some pent-up frustration I'd be more than happy to take out on your face."

His eyes flash yellow again, telling me how much control he lacks. "Try me," his voice is raw, like he's nearly ready to shift, so I step to the side, completely blocking Trix from his line of sight.

"Ronan!" Dax's voice cracks like a command, and I take a step back, whipping my head in his direction.

"What?" I ask, hating that he interrupted my moment.

"Take Trix home."

"Like hell," she sputters. "If anyone gets to hit Chad, it's me."

The man in question snarls, and I shove his chest, hoping he'll turn and leave. I don't want him around Trix, especially when he's this feral.

Can we take a moment to hate his audacity for being impacted by the rejected bond? This fucker doesn't deserve an ounce of kindness.

"I came to talk to you."

Dax eases between him and I, looking at Trix. "Do you want to talk to him?"

She shakes her head and some of the tightness in my chest eases. Of course she doesn't want to talk to him. Why am I so worried?

Probably because he's her fated and there's potential for a life altering bond. It's hard to compete with fate and my friends.

"Well then, that's settled." Dax turns back to Chad, who is vibrating with anger.

"I don't have any food."

"Ronan, get the man some food." Crossing his arms, my friend stands in front of the asshole, daring him to snap or snarl at Trix again.

Self-loathing creeps in because I'm not an alpha, and Chad was ready to brawl with me rather than standing down. I can't protect Trix. Not like she needs.

Reluctantly, and because I have to do what the alpha says, I go to the store. He didn't specify what food to get the prick, so I fill a paper bag full of anchovies, gluten free bread which I know firsthand is dry as hell, and cucumber water.

"Here," I say when I get back, shoving the bag at Chad. "You can go now."

He inspects the contents, scoffing when he sees what I got him, but he's smart enough to keep his mouth shut. "We need to talk soon, Trix."

I step in front of him when he tries to meet her gaze, and point in the direction he came, not bothering to tell him to leave, because he knows he's unwanted.

Good.

The fucker can suffer.

He's an idiot for letting her go, and he's not going to sweet-talk his way into her good graces. I know without a doubt, even though we only met a little over a week ago, Trix would never let him.

And neither would I.

I'll kick his ass every day of the week if I have to in order to keep him away from her.

To protect what's ours.

The thought barrels through my head like a bull, and I take a step back, eyes shooting between Trix and Dax, who are watching me with concern painted across their faces. Who am I kidding? I know she'll never want me like that. I'm worthless.

Fuck. Now I sound pathetic. I can't subject her to how fucked up the inside of my head is. Between my mom and my fated mate, I've been thoroughly ruined.

"Ronan?" Trix asks, and the soft affection I hear there scares the shit out of me.

So I run, ignoring Dax's shouted reminder that my shift is far from over.

I run from the truth, hoping she won't chase after me because I don't think I could deny her answers if she asked me what I'm thinking, and I don't want her to pity me because I'm fucked in the head.

She deserves better.

∼

BELLATRIX

I SHIFT IN CREED'S HOLD WHEN I HEAR THE DOOR OPEN. IT'S late, and Ronan stayed out until he thought I would be asleep, but he doesn't know me as well as he thinks. I thrive on confrontation, and he's not going to get away with disappearing without telling us what the hell he was doing.

He's sure as shit not going to run from me because he's scared.

At first, I thought he'd gone after Chad, but Creed went to look for him and couldn't find any trace of him by the house Chad took over. The way he looked at me before he took off, eyes wide with fright, makes it clear what he was feeling. He was afraid, and I have a sneaking suspicion it has something to do with me and it might explain why he continues to flip from hot to cold. What he told me about his mom makes me so angry, and I think part of his reaction is driven by that.

She fucked with his head, and he doesn't think he deserves affection.

Well, he's about to find out the hard way that I don't give up easily. I mean, if he truly doesn't want me, fine, but I'm going to him and dealing with this now. I've been sick to my stomach wondering where he was and if he'd come back. Not to mention the murderer is still out there.

I bite my lip and nudge Creed. He hums, tugging me closer and sliding his hand over my ass.

"I'm sleepy, but I can be persuaded," he says.

"As tempting as that is, Ronan is here."

His eyes pop open, and we stare at each other in the moonlit room. "You should go talk to him."

The way he understands without me having to explain makes my heart skip a beat. I kiss him, thanking him for being amazing, and slip out of the covers, tossing on one of his shirts and padding to the door.

"Go easy on him."

Turning back to Creed, I nod and head to Ronan's room, which is two doors down from Creed's. Dax is in the middle, but he's on guard tonight. We were all worried about Ronan running off while the killer is still out there, so hopefully he noticed Ronan's return. Creed was supposed to stay with

Dax, but since Ronan was gone, they decided Creed should stay with me.

I don't like the idea of Dax out there by himself, but if anyone is capable of handling danger, it's him.

I knock before I open the door, deciding to give Ronan a fair warning but not giving him the chance to pretend like he's asleep. The lamp on the desk by the door is on, casting a soft yellow glow over the room. He's in the middle of taking off his shirt when I enter, and he pauses, hesitating for a second before ripping it off his head and tossing it on the floor.

No shouting or telling me to leave, so I shut the door and lean against it, watching him as he undoes the button and zipper of his shorts.

"You're staring," he comments, hooking his fingers in the top of them and slowly dragging them down his thick, muscled legs.

I gulp, shamelessly staring at his ass in his boxer briefs. "I heard there was a show."

Turning, his eyes track over Creed's shirt, stopping where the material ends mid-thigh. His hands tug out his ponytail, and he runs his fingers through his thick strands, taking one step forward.

"What are you doing?" he asks, placing his hands on his hips and reminding me it's absolutely not polite to stare at his dick when he's trying to talk to me.

"Where did you go?" I push away from the door and close the distance between us, stopping a few inches away from him and tipping my head back to keep his gaze.

"I needed space."

I bite my lip, studying the little line forming between his eyebrows. "From me?" I guess.

"Maybe."

"Why?" I step closer, making my own breath hitch when our chests brush against one another.

His jaw ticks, and he runs his knuckles over my biceps. "I don't know."

"I didn't peg you for a liar." I go up on my toes, brushing my lips over his cheek and moving to whisper in his ear. "I won't let you run away from me."

I realize that sounds a little psycho, but he needs to know he can't hide from me. We're adults. We can handle this like grown-ups, fucked up parental trauma aside.

"Do you always get what you want?" he asks, a little bit of humor bleeding into his voice.

"Not always." I draw back, lifting an eyebrow at him. "But I know what you want, and I want it too, so, I'm not sure why you ran."

"It's complicated. I don't want to talk."

Fucking fated mates, ruining the fun for the rest of us. I have no doubt he's worried I'll end up rejecting him in some way too.

"Okay," I say, nodding and trying to follow his lead. "What do you want?"

He sighs and grabs my shoulders, slamming his mouth into mine with enough force that we almost knock teeth. I gasp and grab his neck, not letting him pull back. Our lips meet and tongues lock. Heat unfurls in my stomach, races through my blood, and brings forth a moan. His hands grab the backs of my thighs, and I jump up, wrapping my legs around his torso, loving how his muscles are layered with a small cushion of soft skin. He's undeniably strong, but at the same time, he's a teddy bear.

Spinning, he walks us toward the bed, kneeling on it and gently laying me down. I keep my legs locked around him, tugging his middle to meet mine. His cock presses against me, and I writhe beneath him, trying to find the friction I need.

Breaking away from our kiss, he moves back and yanks his boxers off before yanking on my panties. I giggle when he practically jumps back on top of me, but he kisses me again. He moves his hips so his head brushes against my center, but I shove him off of me and onto his back.

"Get over here," he says, but I ignore him and crawl between his legs.

Grabbing his dick, I lower my mouth to his tip, rolling my tongue over it and watching him watch me. His eyes are hooded, and his hips lift off the bed ever so slightly. The best part about giving head is watching them come completely unraveled. I hold his gaze while I take him in, hollowing out my cheeks.

He grunts when I start to bob my head, and his hands fist in my hair. I hum in approval, closing my eyes and moving the fingers I have wrapped at the base of his cock in time with my mouth.

"Trix," he says around a moan, tugging on my hair to get my attention.

I glance at him, and he gives me the sexiest smirk.

"As much as I love seeing you with my dick in your mouth, I want inside of you."

Slowly moving my lips up his length, I pull off with a pop, kissing the very tip of him.

"Maybe next time, my friend."

He laughs at me and lets go of my hair so I can straddle him. "This is why I ran."

Taking my shirt off, I wrinkle my nose at his words. I stroke him and lean forward, hovering my hips just out of reach.

"Because you don't like to come?" I ask, kissing him once before carefully placing him in the right position.

"No," he says, voice strained as I tease him against my entrance. "Because you're unforgettable."

"Good thing we're stuck here together then." I slide down his length, gasping when he drives his hips up, forcing himself the rest of the way in. "Oh fuck."

"You like that?" he asks, doing it again.

"Yeah," I breathe, pinching my nipples and leaning back slightly and grinding down on him.

Our bodies fit together perfectly, like they were made for this moment. His thumb swirls over my clit without warning, and I jerk against him, starting to pick up my pace. He matches me, using the bed as leverage to drive into me from below, his pulsing cock begging me to come all over him.

"Look at me when you come," he demands, and I slam my hands on either side of his head, staring down at him and pressing my body fully against him, grinding and writhing on him.

He grins when I whimper.

"You're so pretty when you take my dick," he growls.

Oh *moons*, I love a dirty talker.

I kiss him, then move my lips to his neck, sucking and biting as his hands find my ass. He squeezes me, spreading them a little and continuing to thrust into me with the force of a wrecking ball.

"You feel so good," he says, moaning when I start to tremble. "Come all over me, beautiful."

"Ronan," I gasp, rolling my hips faster and faster, chasing that warmth building in my core. Chasing that slow tingling starting in my toes, chasing the moans, chasing the throbbing of his cock inside of me until my walls clench around him and I cry out, collapsing against him.

"Fuck," he grunts, holding my hips steady and driving into me so fast all I can do is hold on to him, letting him slam into me again and again until he jerks to a stop, burying himself deep inside of me as he comes.

I lie on top of him, moving my hips back and forth, helping him get it all out and laughing against his chest, kissing his pec before propping myself up on my forearm.

"You'd run away from this?" I ask, giving him a sultry smile.

He shakes his head. "I'm not running again."

"Good," I say, kissing him to cut off anything else he wants to say.

He's not worthless or pathetic.

He's hilarious and sweet and hot as hell.

Ronan is mine.

twenty-one

BELLATRIX

Late the next morning, Ronan and I are sitting at the breakfast bar, laughing at a story he's telling. Dax comes down first, eyeing us with an unreadable look and grabbing his cup of coffee. His night shift ended early, and since Ronan and I were passed out, and Creed had the one the night before, he must have decided to let the next guard shift slide.

"Look at Mr. Silver Fox breaking his own rules," I comment with a grin.

Giving me a look over the rim of his mug, he glares at me. "Next time, I'll send you out there."

"Fine, I told you I'm perfectly capable of helping. Just tell me when and where."

With a grunt, which sort of sounds like a resounding *no*, he sits on my other side, running his hands over his face to try and wake up. The dark circles under his eyes are prominent, and something tells me he hasn't slept since he got in around five this morning.

"You two work it out?" he asks, not a bit bothered by the fact that we had sex.

"I think Ronan came to the realization he can't hide from me." I lean toward Dax. "He definitely likes me," I whisper.

"Can't say I blame him." Dax drinks his coffee, staring me down over the rim of his cup again.

"You're not upset?"

"Nope." He takes another drink. "You're late for your shift," he tells Ronan.

"I know." Ronan rubs his hand over my leg. "This was worth it though."

The corner of Dax's mouth kicks up, and he hums in agreement. "I imagine it was."

Interesting. I expected him to get upset at Ronan for slacking off or at least say something more, but it seems the drill sergeant is learning to bend the rules from time to time without getting curmudgeonly about it.

"The shipment comes in today," he says, changing the topic like we'd been talking about the weather instead of the strange love-square we have going on.

"Need help?" I grin at Creed as he comes into the kitchen with a yawn. "Morning, sunshine."

"Yeah, yeah," he mumbles, ever the morning person, and heads to the coffee.

If anything, coffee will bring us together. At least we can all agree it's a miracle worker.

"You can help if you want. Creed, can you check on the pipe again? I want to make sure the patch is holding."

Creed gives him a thumbs up, opting not to use words just yet as he rests his butt against the counter by the pot of coffee.

"I better go. I'm late for my shift because of you." Ronan tugs a strand of my hair, and I glare at him.

"I didn't make you late. You made that decision."

"Again, worth it." He kisses my cheek and hops off the barstool, flipping the guys off before rushing out of the door.

When I'm done staring after him like some sort of swooning fool, I turn back to my coffee to take a drink, stopping the cup in front of my face when I see the curious look Creed is giving me. He winks at me, and Dax sighs rather dramatically. You'd think he was the woman in the room.

"What?" I ask Dax.

No. Of course I don't sound defensive.

"You might have a magical vagina after all."

I snort and give Dax a look. "Explain yourself, Old Man." Finally, I take a sip. While the coffee isn't great, it's better than nothing and I've grown to like the bitter acidic ways of cheap coffee as of late. The taste resonates with my feelings about Chad.

"You've got my friends wrapped around your pretty little finger."

Setting my cup down, I put my hand on my chest. "You think I'm pretty?" I ask, focusing on the important part. "Thank you."

He scoffs.

"Listen," I say, leaning closer. "Creed and I don't mind sharing." Then a little louder, I say, "Right Creed?" Sliding my gaze to his, I smirk at the wide-eyed expression he shoots me. I can practically hear him screaming *shut up*.

Yeah, he didn't think I noticed how he watched Dax, or how Dax sometimes gives him a look that I know all too well? Well, I'm all about making this happen. I know Creed would be more than excited to hook up with Dax. The thought of them together sets my blood on fire, and I can only hope they'll let me be a part of their first time connecting.

"Is that so?" Dax asks, voice growing husky.

I slip my eyes back to his, watching as they drop to my lips then shoot to Creed. Dax doesn't hide anything, and I hum in approval, a bit too proud of myself for making this a thing. I mean, it's not a thing yet because the thing hasn't happened, but come *on*, it's totally a thing!

"As long as Creed's okay with it," I say, giving him an out. I did push the subject, but ultimately it is up to him on whether or not this happens. I may push him from time to time, but I'd never agree to something he isn't comfortable with.

Dax watches Creed with a heated gaze, and Creed's face grows an adorable shade of scarlet. He takes a drink of coffee, liquid courage and all that, and nods.

"Yeah, I'm good." He avoids Dax's stare, only looking at me.

I smile at him, hopefully letting him know I'd never do anything to hurt him. I wouldn't have mentioned it if I wasn't one hundred percent sure Dax was into it too. He nods in understanding, and I sigh in relief.

"You too scared to say it to me?" Dax asks, drawing both of our attention to him. He's resting his forearms on the bar, leaning over it slightly. In the morning his voice is a little gravelly, and I can't help but wonder how he would sound during sex.

Creed's swallow is audible, but to my surprise, he answers Dax. "I'm good with it, Dax."

"Good with what?" Dax presses, his eyes narrowing to slits.

I want to smack and kiss him all at the same time because he's torturing Creed, but then again, it's incredibly sexy to watch him make Creed squirm.

Finally finding himself again, Creed pushes off the counter he's leaning on and puts his hands on the one in front of us, leaning forward enough to stare directly into Dax's eyes.

"Sharing. You, me, her. I want all of it."

Oh. My. Men. Don't you love it when men, *men*? Ugh. Be still my vagina. I fan myself because the solar panels must be broken or something and the air must be off. I'm on fire right now.

Dax chuckles darkly, slowly lowering his gaze and

checking Creed out. I nearly fall out of my chair when Creed takes in a sharp breath, because fucking hell.

"We'll see about that, Creed." Dax sits back, picking up his coffee and flicking his gaze to me. "See? Magic. Vagina."

I burst out laughing, and they both follow seconds later. They can blame this on me all they like, but if I never showed up, I bet things would have evolved at their own pace. Not at Chaotic Bellatrix pace.

Some people hate chaos, and in turn, end up hating me because they're stuck in between nonexistent lines they think exist in the world, but really the lines are self-imposed. I like when people let me take a giant eraser and free them of their confines, helping them enjoy everything there is to love about life.

If anything, chaos is my gift to the world.

Ronan, Dax, and Creed are fully accepting of me for who I am. And for some reason, my mind whispers that perhaps things are a little too good to be true.

twenty-two

DAX

Casting a sidelong glance at Trix as we head toward the docks, I study her. She's grinning, totally lost in thought. I had a notion Creed might be bi, but she confirmed it today, and I'm relieved. I've been able to maintain the aura of a friend for a while, but my thoughts have been less than friendly about him as of late. The other night didn't help things either. I'm usually better about hiding my desires, but I slipped up.

I've had my equal share of men and women as partners, but coming to the island put me on guard. I definitely didn't want to screw anything up by attempting a connection with Creed when he didn't want it.

Trix had better know what she's doing because this could all go to hell if we're not careful. For some reason though, I find not only myself, but my friends trusting her.

Must be the magic vagina. I scoff and shake my head, biting back a smile at my own joke.

"You have something to say, Old Man?" Turning and giving me a raised eyebrow, she sizes me up.

"Creed and Ronan are like family to me," I say, suddenly needing her to know how much power she's holding.

She stops walking and grabs my arm, halting my steps. "I know." She closes the distance between us, peering up at me. "I'm not trying to destroy what you have. It's okay if you don't want this."

I shake my head. "That's not what I meant. I needed to be sure you knew what was at stake."

"I get it." She puts her hand on my chest. "I'm all in."

Gripping her chin with my thumb, I pull her lips to mine. "Good, because I'm afraid you've gone too far. There will be no escaping us now."

The smile she cracks at my crazy comment reassures me she really does fit with us, and I kiss her again before dropping my hold on her. "The boat is almost here."

BELLATRIX

The guards who arrive don't speak to us. Two of them set crates full of supplies on the dock while the other one watches us with squinted eyes, like he expects us to attack or go rabid at any moment. I move to flip him off, but Dax grabs my arm and pushes it down.

"Don't give them a reason to hurt you," he whispers.

With a huff, I curl my middle finger back to join my others in a fist, hating that they have any power over us at all, but this is the life we're stuck in now. When they finish setting out the supplies, Dax clears his throat.

"No eggs?"

One guard with bushy eyebrows shakes his head. "Maybe next time."

Before Dax can say anything else, the one who'd been watching us starts the boat, drowning us in the sound of the engine as they take off at top speed.

"Assholes!" I scream, even though they probably can't hear me over the roar of the engine and slapping of water.

"It's not worth getting mad about," Dax says, squatting down to grab a few crates.

I grab two, scowling at him. "Everything about this situation is worth getting upset about."

Lifting a shoulder, he shrugs. "If you want to stay angry, that's fine by me, but I can tell you it's not a great life. The island is no vacation, but there are worse ones to be on." He glances over his shoulder at the water. "There are some islands out here that are filled with legitimate psychopaths. They'd make our murderer look like a princess."

"We should write a letter to the elders, make them try to see that we don't belong here. I'm not crazy, well, not in the rejected mate sense. I won't go feral and reveal myself to the humans. I don't think you guys would either."

Sighing as we walk toward the shops, he shakes his head. "It's not that simple. You have to file a formal petition, go through official review and psychoanalysis, and then get High Pack approval. On top of that, you need an alpha to accept you into their pack. Do you know any alphas willing to do that?"

I grimace, because the only alphas I know are assholes. Well, aside from Dax. He's nice. All the rest are jerks who did nothing to stop the shitty treatment my dad got.

"It's not fair," I whisper.

"No. It's not." Dax sets his crates on the ground. We're at the back entrance to the stores where there's a small loading door. He takes a set of keys out of his pocket and opens the door, holding it with his foot and bending to grab his crates. "You can set them on the right."

I do as he says then head off to go get more. In total there are around twenty-four crates. Taking the time to myself, I jog toward the shore, leaving Dax behind. He seems to understand my desire for space, because he keeps his casual pace, letting me pull ahead. Grabbing the next couple of crates, I start the trek back, this time walking.

"Show-off," Dax says when I pass him on the road, grinning at me.

"Can't let you get too cocky," I quip, smiling until he can't see my face, then I let it drop, letting the displeased frown take hold.

I set the load down, wipe my forehead with my arm, and glare at the supplies. I'm sure with time I'll come to feel the same as Dax does, but right now, the entire concept is so fresh it stings. Turning with a huff, I start back for the next load.

"I'll make you dinner." Dax gives me a hopeful look. "Anything to make it better."

I can't help but laugh. "Food will always make me happy."

Smirking, he nods. "It's a date then." He continues on in the opposite direction, and I watch him for a second, gaze slipping down to his perky ass.

I guess the island isn't all that bad.

A twig snaps just as I enter the thick of the trees on my way to the dock. I stop, probably the stupidest thing to do when hearing that sort of sound, and look around. Birds are tweeting, a butterfly flutters past, and a small grouping of gnats swarms off to the side.

Nothing seems amiss.

I'm sure that's what the shifters who died thought too.

Great, now I'm being paranoid.

Trying to shake off my unease, I begin to walk, but something crashes into my side. I scream, but a hard hand clamps down over my lips, silencing all but a sharp squeak. A muscled arm bands around my waist in a vice grip, dragging me into the trees.

I bite the hand, satisfied when a pained grunt comes from the man holding me. He doesn't move his palm though, if anything he shoves it against my skin harder, making it impossible to hold the bite. I relent my grip and opt for slamming my head back, only he dodges the hit.

"Calm the fuck down, *mate*."

Oh. Hell. No.

I know this fucker did not call me his mate. Seething and raging, I rant against his skin, but none of my cursed words come out coherent, and he merely scoffs and picks me up, finally removing his hand from my mouth to spin me around and backhand me. My head whips to the side, and I swallow a cry because I refuse to give him the satisfaction.

"Good. About time you shut the fuck up."

"Let me go." I keep my voice low and calm, but I want nothing more than to scream.

"No. You're mine, or did you forget that already?"

I thrash in his arms. "I'm not yours! I rejected you, you dick."

His laugh makes the hair on my arms rise. "You didn't reject shit, princess. I rejected you."

Only because of a technicality, but I don't bother arguing with him. He stops and spins me around, holding my shoulders so hard I feel my bones grind together. If he's not careful, he'll break something.

"I need you to be mine so I can go home."

Dropping my head back, I let out a loud laugh. "Oh, that's rich. All of a sudden you need a mate?"

"Stop laughing," he snarls with enough violence I close my mouth and peer at him.

His eyes are wild, jumping from my face to the surrounding forest so quickly he looks like he's tweaking out. Is this what they mean when wolves go feral after being rejected?

"Let me go, Chad."

Digging his fingers into my skin, he shakes his head. "Shut up."

"Please—" His lips pull back, revealing sharp teeth. He's partially shifted, and his gaze is trained on my neck. Oh fuck. He's going to try and mark me. I can't let him do that.

"Stop. Chad, don't." I sound pathetic and whiny, but this situation is getting dangerous.

I don't know if the mark will make the bond reinitiate, but I don't intend to find out. He growls and dives for my neck. I try to shove him back, but I can't. He's too strong. His sharp teeth press into my skin.

"Trix!" Dax's voice carries through the trees, making Chad stop.

The sharpened point of his teeth clamp around my pulse point, hard enough to hurt but not to actually bite me. He growls again then rips his face away from my neck, scowling toward the dock.

"Trix, where the hell are you?"

I open my mouth to answer Dax, but Chad picks me up and throws me over his shoulder, and all of my air whooshes out in a hard wheeze. I manage to knee him in the chest, but it does nothing to deter him. When I finally suck in enough air to speak, I slam my fists into his back.

"Let me down, you piece of shit!"

"I said we needed to talk—" His words are cut off when a deep growl sounds from behind him, which is where my head dangles.

I lift my eyes, meeting the angry yellow gaze of a giant gray and white wolf. I don't know who it is, but without a doubt, I know it is one of my guys. No other wolf on this island would look as murderous.

"You done fucked up now, *Chad*." With renewed confidence, I rear back and slam my elbow into the side of his neck. He stumbles slightly, and his grip on my hips loosens enough that I wiggle out of his hold, landing on the ground with an unladylike grunt.

"Douche," I wheeze, staying on my back for a second before hopping to my feet.

Chad is storming toward me. The wolf is at my side in an

instant, snapping razor sharp teeth and growling so deep a shiver skates down my spine. My wolf howls in encouragement inside my head. We hate our mate. He tried to force us into the bond after rejecting us.

He's an asshole, and I bet he has a tiny penis.

Speaking of dick, I glance to the side as Chad nears, holding my hand up to steady the wolf. Yellow eyes flick to mine, and I count down in my head, waiting for Chad to get just close enough before using my enhanced speed to slam my foot into his precious jewels, crushing them with my new Vans. The impact of my kick reverberates up my leg, but I grind my teeth and kick again. Chad curls forward, clutching his groin and crying out in pain.

"Trix!" Dax shouts again from off in the distance.

"I'm here!"

I glance at the wolf. "Thanks for coming to the rescue."

With a yip, the animal darts off into the trees. I frown after him, wondering why Ronan or Creed would choose to run. They helped me after all. Or maybe they're embarrassed I took Chad down when they felt it was their responsibility?

"Motherfucker." Dax skids to a stop next to me, eyes flashing over me before they jump to Chad, who is still writhing on the ground. "I warned you once," he says, then he launches himself on top of Chad.

The downed man barely dodges the first fist, but the second one connects. Then the third and fourth. Somewhere around the tenth, when I hear bones crunch, I grimace and race forward, grabbing Dax's shoulder and yanking him back.

He snarls at me, but I pinch his side. "No. He's had enough. Haven't you, Chad?" The name leaves an acidic taste in my mouth, and he winces when I cut a glacial gaze in his direction.

"I wanted to talk to you," he stammers, as if that explains

why he tried to kidnap and force me into the bond. His left eye is nearly swollen shut, and the rest of his face is one big, purple bruise. Blood is leaking from his split lip, and I can't help but think red is a good color for him.

Shoving in front of Dax, I squat so Chad and I are eye to eye. "I don't know how to make it any clearer for you. I don't want to talk to you. I don't want to breathe the same air as you. I don't want to see you. You're pathetic, and you were never even close to worthy enough for me to call you mate. You are dead to me, do you understand?"

His eyes find the ground, and his jaw twitches in anger, but he nods sharply.

"Good. Now get out of here before I let Dax finish what he started." I rise, moving back to Dax's side.

His arm comes around my waist, dragging me against his side and holding me there. Dax touches my neck, as if he can sense what almost happened. His fingers shake against my skin, so I wrap my hands around him to keep him from going for the douche again.

"I'm okay."

Dax grinds his teeth together, eyes glowing bright yellow. "You need to go. Now." Dax's command rips through the air as he swings his gaze to meet Chad's.

He glances at us, face pinching in frustration, but he's wise enough to listen to the warning tone in Dax's voice. Dax is only a few seconds away from ending Chad entirely. His wolf is too close to the surface, and if he shifts, Chad is fucked.

Dax and I watch him leave; his arm flexes against my stomach as he tries to pull me closer.

"I'm okay," I tell him, craning my neck to look in his eyes. "Thank you for coming to help."

"I should have been here sooner."

I shrug. "Creed or Ronan showed up to scare him off."

"Really?" He glances around.

"The wolf ran."

"What color was it?"

"Gray and white." I give up trying to push out of his hold and decide to lean in, resting my body completely against his. The remaining tension bleeds from my body the longer I stay in his arms, and I let out a soft sigh.

His chest rumbles in approval. "Creed's wolf is brown and Ronan's is black."

"Then who saved me?" Frowning, I chew on my cheek. I was sure it was one of the guys.

"Harlow."

Oh.

I scan the forest, hoping to catch a glimpse of her wolf again, but she's long gone. I make a mental note to go find her later to tell her thanks.

"Should we finish?" I ask, lightly pushing on Dax's chest with my palm.

Finally, he lets go of me.

"There's only one load left to carry. Are you up for helping me organize?" He gives me a careful once-over, and I imagine he's waiting for me to break down.

"Of course," I say, propping my hands on my hips. "It'll take more than a crazy ex-fated to break this woman."

His lips twitch. "Good to hear. Come on, little savage."

My heart flutters at the nickname, and a cheesy grin splits my lips. "I knew you liked me, Old Man."

"Yeah, yeah. Don't let it go to your head." He turns and walks off with a shake of his head, like he's done with my antics.

"Too late," I singsong to his back, practically skipping to catch up to him. I don't complain about how fast he's walking because he did say he liked to be chased.

And damn if I'm not ready to give chase.

twenty-three

BELLATRIX

A while later, after I finish restocking the grocery store with Dax, I head to Harlow's house in the cul-de-sac. Dax didn't want to let me go alone, but he finally agreed to let me go with the condition that he'd walk me and wait for me to walk me back.

Glancing over my shoulder, I flip him off from where he sits on the porch of one of the empty homes, grinning when he scoffs and returns the gesture.

My feet are loud on the steps on purpose. I want to give Harlow plenty of warning that someone is here because she's a little jumpy. Rapping my knuckles on the door four times, I drop my hand and wait, eyeing the dust free porch. She takes good care of the place. I wonder how many times she sweeps on any given day.

It has to be an unhealthy amount because I don't see a speck of dirt or a stray leaf anywhere. The wooden planks look freshly polished, but I don't smell any chemicals to indicate she'd just done so.

The deadbolt snicks back, and she opens the door, eyeing me between the small crack she's created.

"What do you want?" she asks, eyebrows drawing down.

"Really? You can't even let me in? Are you scared of me?" I cross my arms, daring her to stay hidden behind her door.

"You're a pain in the ass," she mumbles, opening the door all the way.

"Ah, there you are. You look good, Harlow. Bite any bastards lately?"

Her eyes pinch at the edges. "Unfortunately, no."

I nod. "Sorry about that. I would have given you your shot, but then you ran off." I hold her guarded gaze. "Thanks for coming to help me, Harlow."

"I didn't do anything." She sniffs, pushing her hair out of her face. "That was one solid kick to the nuts."

Smirking, I chuckle. "Yeah, I don't think he'll be having any kids."

We share a moment, where she's not guarding her thoughts and where I think we might be on the verge of becoming friends, but as quickly as she dropped them, her walls slam back into place and she glances away.

"Is that all?"

"Yeah, I guess so." I grind my teeth and spin on my heel, hating that I'm sad she doesn't want to be friends. Having the guys is nice, but I long for a woman to talk to. I miss my sister now more than ever, because she'd die if I told her what was going on with the men. She'd call me a harlot, squeal in delight, then beg me for details.

A wave of sadness threatens to pull me under, but I shove that shit down and slam a lid on top of it because if I let it out, I'll fall apart, and I'm not going to do that. Crying won't change my situation, so I opt for the only thing that makes me feel like a goddess.

"Hey, Old Man," I call when I reach the sidewalk of the house where he's waiting. "Let's make a bet."

He narrows his eyes. "On what?"

Edging toward the road, I shoot him a sultry wink. "I beat you to the house, you have to do whatever I want."

"And when I win?" he asks, as cocky as ever. "What do I get?"

I shrug. "I guess that's your decision. On three?"

Nodding, he joins me on the sidewalk in a few quick steps.

"One." I sprint toward the house, cackling when he curses.

"That's cheating!"

"Who gives a shit?" I shout over my shoulder. "Try to keep up, Dax!"

I'm taunting him, knowing full well I'm about to get my ass handed to me, because while he may be older, he's an alpha and faster than me.

"That ass is going to be red when I'm done with it."

"I'm counting on it!" I pump my arms as hard as I can, but Dax passes me in a matter of seconds, a deep rumbling laugh bursting out of him when he glances at me.

"Come on, little savage. You can do better than that."

I scowl at him, pretending to be annoyed, and push myself to go faster. It's no use though, because he still beats me with seconds to spare. When I reach the steps to the house, he grabs me around the waist and tosses me over his shoulder like a barbarian. It reminds me of what happened with Chad, only I don't feel scared, and I know Dax won't hurt me.

"Really?" I ask, propping my elbows on his back and holding my chin in my hand. "This is a bit primal, don't you think?"

"Hardly, but we can get a little wild if you want." He smacks my ass, suddenly remembering his promise to me. "Maybe not today though."

He runs his palm over the globe of my butt, fingers grazing over my core. I stifle an embarrassing moan as he carries me through the door and up the stairs to his room.

Ever so slowly, he slides me down his body, his heated gaze eating up every inch of me before coming to meet mine.

"You said you wanted to be chased," I say, smiling at him.

His eyes dance with mirth, and he steps into me, forcing me to step back. "I did say that, didn't I?"

Nodding, I reach for him, but he grabs my hands and wrenches them behind my back. "Naughty little savage."

I pout, and he captures my lip with his teeth, tugging on my bottom lip softly before kissing me so deeply he steals the breath from my lungs. His lips caress me, promising a slow, tortuous sort of pleasure as he shows me just how skilled he is with his tongue. I try to get a hand out to grab him, but his hold tightens on my wrists, restraining me.

Pulling away, he rests his forehead against mine. "Here's the deal, Trix. If this is happening, you have to give me the control."

"Of course," I say, reaching for another kiss, but he rears back.

"Total control. Can you do that?"

I bite my lip, eyes bouncing between his. He's completely serious, and for some reason, my heart skips a beat at the thought of giving up any power to him. Sex is my safety net, the thing I can go to and know I'll be able to ground myself. Part of the grounding comes from being in charge, whether giving head or controlling the pace while on top, my power comes from that.

I don't have to be in charge of an entire sexual encounter, but I like to have some control during the act. What he's asking is for something I've never done. Completely putting myself at his mercy and hoping he can bring me the same sort of grounding is a big step, but there's something so sure in his eyes, I find myself nodding.

"Yes," I rasp, throat constricting as if to stop the word altogether.

"Good," he says, face darkening. "Now, take off your clothes."

Instead of stepping away, he stays close, making me press

against him when I arch my back as I pull my shirt off. His fingers barely touch my stomach, making me shudder as I reach up and undo my bra. Holding his fiery gaze, I slip off my shorts and underwear, wondering how undressing can turn me on so much.

"Lie on the bed."

Swallowing, I take backward steps until I reach the bed, watching him devour my naked flesh with his eyes. I scoot back, resting my head on his pillow so I can watch him.

He uses one hand to yank his shirt off then drops his pants and boxers with practiced ease. His thick thighs flex when he steps toward me. One of his hands strays to his erection, and he grabs hold of his shaft, stroking it once and releasing a dark chuckle when I bite my lip.

"Touch yourself," he commands, stopping at the edge of the bed.

"Like this?" I ask, cupping my breasts and kneading them.

He tsks. "Not there."

Not needing further instruction, I slip one hand down my torso and dip my fingers between my folds, teasing my clit before pushing two inside of my pussy.

"Good girl. Show me how you come."

I bite my cheek, flames licking up my neck at how hot and bothered he's making me, and give him exactly what he wants without an ounce of shame. I tug on my nipple and pull my fingers out of my wet core, using the lubrication to circle the sensitive bundle of nerves, Pushing and pressing and teasing until a tremble works up my spine.

Dax puts his hands on the mattress, leaning over me, gaze focused on my fingers. He licks his lips, flicking his eyes to meet mine with a devilish grin splitting his lips.

"Stop."

"What?" I ask in annoyance, not listening because I'm so close.

"Stop or this ends."

Fuck.

With a soft growl, I rip my fingers away from my clit and huff.

"Good." He crawls over me, and for a few seconds I think he might give in and give me exactly what I need, but he doesn't enter me.

Instead, he drives his thigh between my legs, using his forearms to hold most of his weight off of me. Ever so gently, his skin meets my core. I arch my back at the contact. I was so close to coming before he made me stop.

"Rub against me."

With a slight furrow of my brow, I lift up, grinding my pussy against his thigh. He's still grinning, enjoying torturing me a bit too much. The next time I press myself against him, he pushes back, working his leg up and down, dragging his flesh against my core.

"Fuck," I gasp, practically humping his leg at this point, but he doesn't seem to mind. At least he doesn't until I part my lips, preparing to release a soft cry. I'm so close.

He moves his leg on the other side of mine, lowering his face to mine. "Not yet, little savage."

"There better be an orgasm involved or I may kill you."

Laughing, he nudges my cheek with his nose. "Turn over."

Scowling at him to let him know how I feel, I roll my eyes but do as I'm told all the same because I told him I'd give him control. He doesn't think I'll listen, and I hate being wrong. So as much as I want to take my orgasm from him, I comply and wait for him to give it to me.

"Slip your hands between yourself and the mattress and make two fists."

He shifts, body lowering, hovering over mine but never exactly touching me. His breath brushes against the back of my neck, making me shiver.

"Now, Trix."

I lift my hips slightly, placing my fisted hands against myself.

"There you go. Now work that sweet little pussy."

Burying my head into his pillow, I writhe against my fisted hands, surprised to find my clit warming in approval. My breaths are coming in pants as I basically hump my hands, wondering all the while why I've never tried this before.

"That's enough," he says, earning another huff of frustration from me. "Roll over."

I turn, lying on my back, hair splaying around me in a mess of tangles, and I narrow my eyes on him. "This is annoying."

"For you," he says, brushing his lips over mine. His teeth grab my bottom lip, tugging hard before releasing it and sucking it between his, swirling his tongue over the pain. "I'm enjoying myself." He lowers his body another inch until I can feel the tip of his cock brushing against my stomach. "Watching your pupils dilate and hearing your heartbeat spike when you almost come, and then enjoying how mad you get when I make you stop."

"At least one of us is happy," I grumble, not entirely mad, because part of me is enjoying this game.

"You'll be happy too," he says, finally resting his weight against me. His hands hold the back of my head, and he kisses me, stealing gasps and whimpers with his tongue. When he rocks his lower body against mine, I try to maneuver my hips into the right position. "I told you, Trix. You're not in charge."

He lifts off of me, and I almost burst into a stream of curses, but his mouth clamps onto my clit, tongue fucking me with an unrelenting, almost punishing pace. I grab his hair, trying to work my pussy against his face, but he yanks my hands away, holding them in one hand and wrenching them to the side. His other arm presses into my stomach, easing my hips back down as his fingers wrap around one of my arms to hold me in place.

"Relax," he whispers against me, burying his head between my legs, tongue working into me and licking my walls in languid laps. He licks me from my opening to my clit, humming as he wraps his lips around me again.

"Dax," I beg, desperately trying to grind against him. "Please."

Lifting his gaze to meet mine, he removes his mouth from my body. "You're so impatient." Then he licks between my slit again, circling my clit with the tip of his tongue a few times until my eyes snap shut, stars bursting across the black I find there. He releases my hands, and I immediately bury them in his hair, shoving him against myself like a desperate bitch, but it doesn't stop him from making me tremble beneath him.

My toes curl, tingles racing through my body as he continues to work my clit, pushing me past the point where my blood heats, fire sweeps through me, and where my words make any sense. Chest rising off the bed, my jaw drops open and I moan his name, earning a cocky whisper of a chuckle against my skin as he cleans up my cum, licking it up like I'm his favorite meal.

"There she is," he says when my hands drop to my sides and he pulls away, gaze skating over my face. "Now you get what you want." Crawling up the bed, he positions himself between my hips. "Pinch your nipples."

I grab my tits, rolling my hard nubs between my fingers and pinching them like he said. His cock eases inside of me, the V of his stomach tightening right before he slams all the way in, sliding in without any resistance.

"Oh fuck," he moans, holding himself deep inside of me and taking a deep breath. "Fuck."

"Mmm," I say in agreement. "Feels like home."

He nods, grabbing my hips and lifting them off the bed so he can slam me against his dick. "Hold on to the headboard."

Reaching back, I wrap my fingers around the bar at the bottom. He grunts as he pistons into me, slamming against my G-spot over and over until my walls are throbbing and my pussy weeps over him, soaking his shaft with cum and begging him for more all at the same time.

"So. Fucking. Perfect." He drops my hips, laying his chest over mine as he goes deeper than ever, barely moving his hips as he hits that perfect spot again, this time gently coaxing me toward another orgasm.

"Can I kiss you?" I ask, remembering he's supposed to be the one in control and I can't force his mouth to mine if I want him to continue.

"Of course, little savage." His mouth captures mine, our tongues tangling and battling for control. Instead of my usual demands, I soften against him and take a slow, languid taste of him, following his lead. His hips pull back a little farther, slamming back inside of me hard enough I gasp into his mouth.

Breaking away from our kiss, he moves his lips to my neck, kissing down my throat. "You're so beautiful when you fall apart." He slams into me again. "So pretty when those walls squeeze my dick and beg for more." Another hard thrust. "So intoxicating when those lips part and moan my name."

He continues to praise me, beating my pussy with his cock after each compliment, as if he wants me to remember his words when I feel the aftershocks of his thrusts tomorrow. He wants me to remember how he made me give up control. To remember how he gave me these orgasms instead of me taking them from him.

"Good," he growls into my ear, "girl." His hips slam into mine, and in an unexpected move, his hand finds its way into my hair, and he yanks my head back, drawing a throaty moan from me when the slight pain amps up the pleasure. His teeth clamp over my pulse point, replacing Chad's marks with his own and biting down as he wrecks me with his dick. I scream his name and his own cry is muffled against my skin as he thrusts and stills, dick pulsing inside of me as he fills me with his cum, marking me with his scent and leaving yet another reminder of who owned who in this encounter.

Dax.

Dax made me his bitch, and I'd gladly do it again, because my core throbs from his sweet torture, and my heart is racing faster than it possibly ever has before.

"Good girl," he murmurs again.

A ridiculous smile creeps over my face, but I don't try to hide it.

This was exactly what I needed.

twenty-four

CREED

Dropping the last of the tools into the portable tool box, I lock the gate to the water main. The patch is holding and there are no new leaks, so that's a good sign. The last thing we need is for our water supply to have issues. I turn to grab my things, but stop halfway when I spot Chad. His face is beat to hell, and he's holding his nuts like he's in pain. Without even needing to know the details, I know he's done something stupid.

Something violent and dark rises within me the closer he gets. The road to the house he's taken residence in passes by this one. I can't tell if he's noticed me because his eyes are swollen. Deciding to make it known that I'm here, I take the ten steps from my road to the middle of his, stopping directly in his path.

He stops, shoulders bunching and fingers fisting at his sides. "I don't want any trouble."

Studying the discoloration on his face, I take a step forward. "Is that so?"

"Yeah," he grits between clenched teeth.

He's an alpha, so by nature, he's stronger and faster than me, but the rage building within me blinds me to the facts. Whatever natural advantage he has doesn't surpass the unbridled emotions welling within me.

"If you hurt her—"

"She's fine. Your alpha friend did this to my face." He

waves his hand in front of himself.

"And you think that's all you'll get?" I ask, taking another step to close the distance between us.

"Really? You're going to kick my ass without even knowing what happened? Your asshole of a friend attacked me practically unprovoked. No wonder they send rejects to these islands. Guys like you give us a bad rap."

"Here's the thing," I say, taking another step, stopping a foot away from him. "Dax is the most level-headed alpha I've ever met. He doesn't do shit unprovoked, so whatever happened, you deserved it."

Before he can ask me what he deserves, I move, side stepping a fist he throws up on instinct and jamming my palm into his nose, breaking it on impact. Blood gushes from his nostrils, coating his mouth and chin. He shouts in pain and swings for me again, but he really is beat to hell.

The idiot could have shifted and healed himself, but apparently his mind was preoccupied. Knowing who preoccupies his mind makes me all the more angry, so I bring my foot up and slam it into his stomach, knocking him back.

"You're an idiot if you think we will let you anywhere near Trix."

"She's my fated," he growls, collapsing to the pavement and holding his stomach.

"You rejected her. She's your nothing."

A mocking laugh falls from his reddened lips. "And you're her, what? You're not mates."

Heat rushes through me, kindling an already red hot fire. I launch myself at him, but arms wrap around my middle and yank me back.

"Easy, Creed. He's trying to get a reaction because he knows Trix is ours and it's killing him." Ronan takes a few steps back, putting more space between us and the bastard. "If you want to have some semblance of a normal life on this island, I suggest you erase all thoughts of Trix from your mind. Otherwise, I'll let my brothers kill you for your stupidity."

We don't call each other brothers often, because we're not blood, but the time we've spent together on this island has formed an undeniable bond between me, him, and Dax. They're the family I pick.

And so is Trix.

Chad shoves off the ground, rising to his feet with a groan. "You're going to regret touching me." He scowls at us and storms away, finally shifting and shredding his clothes in the process.

Ronan releases me once Chad is racing up the steps of his house. We stare after him, and I imagine Ronan is thinking the same that I am.

Chad doesn't get to touch her.

He doesn't get to think about her.

Or he'll find his stay at Wolfsbane Island cut short.

∽

BELLATRIX

Sometime during Dax and I hooking up, Creed came home. The downstairs shower is running when I go to grab water after Dax falls asleep, so I decide to sit and wait for Creed to finish to see what his plans for the day are. Dax has to switch shifts with Ronan in a few hours, and since their shifts rotate, the guys always benefit from naps.

I sit in Ronan's chair, eyeing the game of solitaire he has going on to see if I can help him out. Bringing my eyebrows down, I study the cards like I know what I'm doing. Who the hell am I kidding? I never bothered to learn how to play this game because it takes forever.

Moving my hand over a card, I stop short when the bathroom door opens. I shoot my gaze in that direction, grinning at Creed when he enters the kitchen with nothing but a towel wrapped around his waist.

"Hey, Creep." My fingers brush over a card. I think if I move this one on top of the queen of hearts, it'll make a stack. That's what they're called right? Stacks?

Fuck. I suck at this game. Glancing back at Creed, I pick the card up, deciding to try it anyway.

He tries to be mad at the nickname, but his grin reveals that he loves it. "Hey, Trix. Ronan will be pissed if you mess his game up."

Pausing before I set the card down, I wrinkle my nose. "Like *hey, that was my spot* mad or *that's my girl you're flirting with* mad?"

"Definitely that's my girl."

With a heavy sigh, I return the card to its respective place and lean back in the comfy computer chair, setting my arms on the rests.

"How was your morning? Get your work done?"

He nods, going to a cabinet and grabbing one of the granola bars. I lift my eyebrows and pout my lip, hoping he'll take mercy.

"You know, you can use your words." He grabs another one and tosses it to me.

"True, but I like how you understand me without me having to say anything."

"Damn puppy dog eyes." He rips the wrapper and takes a bite. "Saw your boyfriend."

I give him a look. "I think you're trying to be funny, but I kind of want to dunk your head in the toilet if you're referring to Chad as my boyfriend."

Swallowing, he grabs a cup and fills it with water from the tap. "Fine. I ran into the douchebag. He was pretty beat up."

"Was he?" I ask, drumming my fingers on the arms of the chair.

He nods and tips his head to the side.

"See, I can read you too. You want me to tell you what happened, but you're dancing around the subject when you could have just asked me directly."

Rolling his eyes, he drinks his water, waiting for me to break and tell him everything.

It takes about three seconds for me to finally tell him everything that happened.

"Definitely deserved it then." He sets the cup down and walks around the counter, coming to stand in front of me. "Are you hurt?" His finger touches my cheek which is still red from the slap.

"My face hurts a bit from his backhand, but I'll survive. What did he deserve?"

He doesn't answer.

"Creep. Did you defend my honor?"

Placing his hands on the top of the chair, he leans over me. I lift my gaze to meet his and bite my lip, trying to avoid staring at his abs.

"What if I did?" He's not smiling.

He's worried about how I'll react.

"Well," I say, reaching for him and putting my hand on the back of his neck. "Then I say thank you for kicking his ass." I kiss him and smile against his lips. "You're also really sexy when you get serious."

Finally he laughs, breaking the tension and straightening. My hand may or may not grope him on the way back to my lap.

"I'm going to get dressed. Do you want to play Stratego after?"

"Do cows shit?"

He looks confused for a second.

"The answer is yes," I stage whisper, giggling when he tries to pinch me. "Go get dressed before I attack you."

"Don't threaten me with a good time." With a saucy wink he leaves the room.

"NO FUCKING WAY," HE MUTTERS ABOUT TWO HOURS LATER.

I cackle, revealing where I hid my flag. His red pieces are scattered all over the side of the board. My blue pieces are lying around too, but I didn't lose nearly as many as he lost during our third battle.

"I try not to be cocky, really, I do, but I'm a badass at Stratego."

"I didn't think you'd know how to play," he mumbles, picking up his fallen soldiers.

"You put up a good fight." I line up my players, studying them and trying to find a new strategy.

My dad taught me how to play, and while I may not have beaten him very often, I picked up a lot of tricks. These guys are going to be disappointed when they learn I'm claiming the title *Game Night Master*, because every family needs one, and it's clear none of them are qualified.

"That little grin makes me want to kiss you and choke you all at the same time," he says, narrowing his eyes as he sets a piece in a square.

"Why not both?" I ask, deciding on my new plan of attack and grabbing my bombs.

The important part about this game is to work your opponent over. Pay attention, like an engrossed level of attention, to the pieces that aren't your flag when you're setting them up on the board, making them think that's the piece they should focus on. Works like a charm every time.

Well, unless I'm playing against my dad. He knows my methods a little too well.

Sighing, I lose focus on bluffing Creed out and my thoughts turn to my family. On autopilot, I set up my pieces, wondering what they're doing and if they ended up staying with Pack Ozark and if my dad is being treated well. I also worry about my sister. She's a lot softer than I am, and I'm not there to protect her if she needs it.

"Hey," Dax says, startling me out of my thoughts. "You okay?"

He's standing by my chair, searching my face. Creed is staring at me too, a hard line creasing his forehead.

"Yeah. I was thinking about my family."

Understanding blooms over Creed's face and Dax nods, like he suspected where my mind was.

"It gets easier with time," he says. "We're here if you need to talk."

"I'm okay," I say, not wanting to bore them with my feelings. "We loved game night, and it made me think of them. That's all."

"You get a pass for lying because you're beautiful and I'm late for switching shifts with Ronan." Dax leans down and kisses me. "But at some point, you're going to want to talk about it, and we'll be here."

"Such a smooth talker," I joke when he pulls back. "I hear you."

He nods, tweaks my nose, grins at my immediate scowl, and flips Creed off.

"You've got the night shift. See you later." Dax leaves us to our game.

"Okay, Creep. Try not to cry this time." I make my first move, waggling my eyebrows at him.

"You're such a shit talker," he says with a laugh. "Did you get your bad mouth from your dad or your mom?"

"Both," I say, watching him move his first piece. "But when it comes to games, my dad was the biggest crap talker."

"He sounds like a lot of fun."

I hum, agreeing but discouraging further conversation because it hurts too much when I may never see them again. We fall into a companionable silence, playing the game and occasionally throwing a verbal barb.

All the while, I think: this can't be the rest of my life, can it?

twenty-five

RONAN

I make a detour through town, casually—in a very obvious, threatening sort of way—strolling by Chad's residence. It's a little before six at night, and I see a light on inside. Lingering around the front yard for a bit, I wait until my presence is known. When the curtains finally move and he peers out, I lift my hand to say hello.

He scowls. I grin.

He flips me off. I blow him a kiss.

He closes the curtains. I head home.

Perhaps I'm being a bit childish, but it's been a while since I've had a woman to care about, and my battered heart is already attached to her. She's not my fated, but she's hilarious, sexy, and caring. She might be a tad bit reckless, but that draws me in as well.

Bellatrix isn't going to be pushed around by this douche. He can learn his place the easy way or the hard way. It's up to him.

As soon as I reach the house, I hear Creed shouting. I rip the door open and race inside, stopping short when I find him pinned to the ground under Trix. Her hair is a mess and her eyes are wild when they swing up to meet mine.

Creed cackles, earning a slap to the stomach from Trix.

"What the hell is going on?" I ask

"Creep here thought he could cheat." Trix narrows her eyes on him and leans closer. "Didn't you?"

He grins. "How else was I supposed to win?"

"By not cheating!" she yells, but she's not angry. Laughter colors every word, lightening the tone and making him burst into chuckles.

"I-" I shake my head. "Do you want me to kick his ass?" I ask her, raising my fists to show her I'm ready.

Her eyes widen, and she sniffs. "You'd do that for me?"

"Absolutely." The word is out without a second thought, and her head rears back as if she wasn't expecting the severity of my proclamation.

"Are we talking about more than Creed?" She glances between us. "Tell me what happened."

Creed and I exchange looks.

"Chad and Creed might have gotten into a squabble."

"A squabble?" she asks in disbelief. "What are you, eighty?"

"Maybe." I shrug, playing up the whole immortality bit until her face turns scarlet with embarrassment. "No, I'm not eighty. Chad met Creed's palm. His nose may or may not have been broken."

"Definitely broken," Creed cuts in. "And he met my foot."

"He met mine too," Trix says, smirking at Creed. "You guys are the best."

"Aw, sweet cheeks. We like you too."

Her smile falls. "I take it back. Don't call me sweet cheeks."

Waggling my eyebrows, I go to the fridge and open it, trying to manifest something amazing, but nothing appears. "Or what?"

She hops off of Creed and marches over to me. "I may be little, but I'm mighty."

"That ass is mighty," I say, reaching out to smack it.

Squealing, she swats my hand away and covers her butt with her palms.

"None for you."

I slam the fridge shut and prowl toward her, grinning when she immediately steps back upon my approach. "Is that a challenge?"

Sighing, she rolls her eyes. "Are you hungry?"

"Always, but don't change the subject."

"I was joking, Big Guy."

Grabbing the back of her neck, I kiss her hard and release her in the next breath. "Good."

She holds her chest, like her heart is going to burst out of it, and huffs.

"What if we make something together?" I ask as a peace offering, giving her the easy out of this mock argument.

"That works." She opens the pantry and grabs the bag of rice. "What about chicken and rice?"

"We're out of chicken," Creed says. "But I can go get some from the store." He jumps up from the floor and leaves.

"They can send chicken but not eggs?" She shakes her head. "I don't understand the High Pack."

"That makes two of us." I grab a pan and fill it with two cups of water, then dump a cup of rice in and set it on the stovetop.

Trix frowns, watching me as I cross my arms and lean against the counter next to her.

"Sometimes I forget why I'm stuck here, and other times it hits me in the face so hard I see stars."

Grimacing, I search her face. "I wish I could tell you something that would make it better, but I don't know if any of my words will be adequate. It sucks here, but with the right people, it's not so bad."

She nods. "Yeah. You guys make it easier."

We grow quiet, both of us lost in our thoughts until the front door bangs open a few minutes later. "Chicken has arrived!"

"All right, let's get meat ready." Clapping her hands and rubbing them together, she smiles at him like nothing is wrong. The switch from honest to putting on a front is jarring.

"Trix," I say, waiting until she looks at me before I continue, "It's okay to not be okay. You don't have to pretend with us."

"I'm not pretending with you," she says. "I'm pretending for myself, because I don't want to cry."

"We won't run away if you do." Creed hugs her to his side, and she ducks her head and wipes her cheeks.

"Ugh, okay. Chicken." She eyes him. "You're a breast man, no?"

And like that, the tension is dispelled and Creed laughs.

"You know it."

She rolls her eyes and sets to work prepping the meat. Creed brought breasts and thighs because I love dark meat, so she sprinkles all of it with salt and pepper, adding a dash of lemon pepper to the mix to give it a little extra flavor.

Creed leans against the counter by the breakfast bar, and together we watch her work, laughing at the jokes she cracks to keep herself from getting too serious.

Trix is strong, but I hope in time she'll feel comfortable enough with us to fall apart and let us hold her. We may not be able to make it better, but at least she won't be alone.

twenty-six

BELLATRIX

Another two weeks pass without incident. The guys and I fall into a steady pattern. I switch beds depending on who works the night shift or who needs my attention, and they make me laugh, give me copious amounts of orgasms, and we take care of each other.

Nothing builds a stronger bond than sitting with someone and doing absolutely nothing and still finding a way to enjoy the time spent. Creed and I play games. Ronan and I talk about our lives before the island while he plays solitaire. Dax and I sit in the guard station together, watching the birds fly through the trees and making sure everyone has what they need.

I see Harlow a few times. She smiles and says hi, but for the most part she keeps to herself and maintains her distance. Aside from when the other shifters come to get their supplies, I don't interact with them. The men, who I've learned are all introverted, don't say much, but they always give my guys a respectful nod. For the most part, they avoid looking at me. I don't know if that's because it's obvious that the guys have staked their claim, or because they're messed up from their broken bonds.

Chad, on the other hand, well, Chad avoids looking at me because he's an asshole. It seems he's traded trying to get my attention with provoking my men. Dax ignores him for the most part, and aside from one tense interaction a few days ago, no fights have broken out. The tension is building though, and I know it's only a matter of time before Chad does something stupid and forces my guys to take matters into their own hands.

On Saturday morning, Dax and I set out on a walk. Creed is watching over the shops and Ronan is sleeping off his night shift. We decide to avoid a chance encounter with Chad and head toward the dock, walking through the path between the trees instead of on the road.

"The morning sun looks good on you."

Shooting Dax a funny smile, I gaze up at the sky. "Thanks."

"Your smile is gorgeous."

"Are you trying to get in my pants?" I ask in mock outrage.

He chuckles and looks away, biting his bottom lip. "There will be no trying, Trix."

Gasping, I clutch my imaginary pearls and fan my face. "Men like you are the reason women swoon."

We change direction slightly to continue toward the dock.

Bringing his gaze back to meet mine, his eyes darken, then suddenly shoot over my shoulder and widen. A growl works up his throat, and I prepare for Chad to say something stupid. Dax grabs my arm and pulls me behind him, turning me in the process. As soon as I'm facing the same direction he's looking, I see Chad.

Only he's not here for a fight.

A few feet over, Chad is lying face down in the dirt. Dax and I race over to him, staring at the gore. Blooms of blood spread across his back, seeping through his shirt. His arms are tied to the back of his head, and his veins are discolored, like the man who died on the dock. He was poisoned too. I register all of this before my mind acknowledges what I see next. On the ground, carelessly tossed on the grass next to his body, is his severed dick. Limp, covered in blood, and clearly cut off with a serrated knife because the skin around the base is not clean cut.

"I think I might throw up," I say, unable to look away from the bloody appendage.

If it were any other time, I'd be thankful he isn't my fated because of the size, but that's not a normal thought to have right now.

So instead, I pull my gaze away and stare at Dax. He's grown pale, probably worrying about his own manhood like men do, but he shakes off his disgust, squatting down to gently roll Chad over.

His body turns over in a rigid way that makes my stomach turn. I take a few steps away, clutching my belly. This is more violent than the other dead body I'd seen only weeks before.

Stab wounds litter his body, covering his stomach, thighs, and a big slash colors his neck scarlet. There's a note taped to his forehead, and Dax, who is made of steel in this moment, carefully reaches up and pulls the paper loose.

He opens the letter, glancing back at me when he's done. His forehead wrinkles and his mouth tugs down.

"If you weren't in the house last night, I'd think this was you." Extending his arm, he waits for me to take the note.

I reach for it, stepping forward to grab it then immediately putting distance between myself and the body. Staring at the paper, I read the words.

Good thing this dick has a tiny prick. He got what he deserved.

The writing is sprawling and loopy, most likely a woman's. Some men write this way, but most don't. It's also highly unlikely a guy cut off Chad's dick. Sure, it's possible, but the penis is sacred to men. A woman, on the other hand, isn't as attached to the appendage. Especially if she feels scorned.

Dax is watching me work through my thoughts with a grimace. "I don't want to say it…"

"You don't have to," I say, folding the note and sticking it in my pocket.

Before I can tell him that I agree, Harlow is the most likely suspect, a whir of an engine slices through the air. Dax is up and sprinting toward the dock in a matter of seconds. I'm not far behind, anything to get away from the sight of Chad's brutally murdered body.

I hated that man. I despised how he rejected me. Why he rejected me. I even enjoyed watching Dax kick his ass, but I didn't kill him. I wouldn't ask the guys to do that either. To me, the best way to hurt him was to let him live and know I was happy without him.

He was the miserable fuck.

But none of that matters now because he's dead.

And Harlow is the murderer.

twenty-seven

DAX

There are two guards on this boat, and I'm relieved to see neither is the douche who came the other two times. I scream at them and wave my arms, drawing their attention. One grabs his gun out of his holster, and the one driving turns the boat and slows it, heading toward the dock.

Trix's breath is accelerated, and her heart is racing. I reach for her hand and pull her to my side, hoping my touch will help her relax. When the guards tie their boat to the post, they hop out and glance around, checking for signs of an ambush before they finally look at me.

"Someone has been murdered."

"Where?" the one who was driving asks.

"Over here." I turn and lead them to where we found Chad, holding Trix's hand the entire way.

"Shit," the other guy mutters. "What the fuck?"

"Yeah." I swallow, avoiding the severed penis. "Are you guys ever going to help us investigate these or does the High Pack really not give a shit?"

"These? There's been more than one?" The driver squints at me, trying to suss out if I'm lying to him.

"Are you new? We've reported the other two. This is the third." I gesture to Chad. "Whoever is doing this needs to be taken care of."

Trix squeezes my hand and shifts closer. I breathe her in, trying to get a handle on my irritation. I'm still pissed the

High Pack is so nonchalant about the deaths. I knew they looked down on us, maybe even pitied us, but for them to not give a damn that shifters are dying under their thumb is another level of coldhearted.

"I'm not new," the guy mumbles, studying Chad's body with a closer eye. "Who did you tell?"

"Dean, or whatever the fuck his name is. The High Pack hasn't sent anyone to help because of your fucked-up priorities," I say.

The guards share a look, brows furrowing. The driver shakes his head.

"There's not a Dean on the guard that we know of."

"Whatever, maybe that wasn't his name, but he knew and he asked for investigators to come help us."

Trix scoffs. "He never told anyone."

We all swing our gazes in her direction, watching as she seethes.

"If you didn't know about this and the name he gave us isn't actually his name, then he never told anyone." She searches my face. "The High Pack doesn't know."

"I assure you, if someone had told us about murders there would have been an official inquiry. You said there'd been two others?" He and his friend squat down, studying the lacerations. "All the same?"

"Not exactly." I explain how we'd found the other two men, both killed in different ways. The only thing consistent was the silver nitrate used to make the death permanent.

"Any idea who might have done this?" The guard looks at me then slides his gaze to Trix. "I dropped him off, and his file said this guy's fated was on this island. Maybe she was pissed and decided to get rid of him for good?"

She bristles at my side. "I was his fated," she confesses. "I didn't do this."

Their gazes drop to our interlocked fingers, and I stiffen. "She was at our house all night."

"Our house?"

"I live with two friends. Trix was there all night. She didn't do this."

One gives me a suspicious once-over. "And what about you?"

"He didn't do it." Trix lifts her chin. "We may know who did it, but it's only a hunch."

"And who do you think it is?" The driver stands, turning away from the body.

"I think we'll talk to the investigators, that is if you're actually going to tell the High Pack and send them."

Scoffing, he eyes the trees. "Yeah, okay. You can wait for the investigators. Expect someone within the hour. Don't move the body and don't touch anything."

Nodding at his buddy, they head to the boat.

"What the hell?" Trix says under her breath as the boat takes off. "How could they not know?"

"I wonder who that guard is."

She gives me a look. "A jackass."

Nodding in agreement, I look toward Harlow's house. "Should we go find her?"

"I don't know. We aren't one-hundred percent sure it was her, and what if we spook her and she runs?"

"She can't go far."

"No, but she could swim out to the second buoy and hurt herself."

"I don't think she'd do that," I say, pulling my mouth to the side.

"Sometimes running is easier than facing the conse-quences of your actions, so I think we wait and see what happens."

Nodding, I tug her toward the house. We need to find

Creed and Ronan before the investigators arrive. That is, if they even show up.

For all we know, the guards were lying.

BELLATRIX

About an hour and a half later, the purring of an engine can be heard near the shops. The guys and I exchange worried glances but decide to stick to the plan. Dax will go with Creed to talk to the investigator, and I'll stay with Ronan.

Climbing the ladder to the platform, Ronan and I settle in for a shift. Knowing something ten times more exciting is happening not so far away makes focusing hard. Hardly anyone comes to the shops anyway, but Dax is adamant that we need to be here.

It makes sense, I guess; serial killers on the loose could lead to chaos, which could turn into looting and violence from the few shifters left on Wolfsbane Island. When it comes to life or death, people typically think about themselves first. That sort of mentality can be dangerous, especially if panic starts to build. So far, everyone has seemed rather disturbingly calm about what has been going on.

I suspect things are going to change once word gets out about how Chad was murdered. Ronan leans forward, resting his forearms on the railing as two men amble down the road, eyes trained on the road leading to the dock.

"Morning," Ronan calls.

They stop, hesitating and shooting their gaze up to the guard tower.

"What's going on?" one asks.

"Another murder." Ronan clicks his tongue and eyes them. "The High Pack sent an investigator."

"Investigator?"

"Yeah." Ronan tips his head to the side. "Worried?"

A tense moment passes. "Let us know if you need anything," the guy finally says, nudging his friend.

They turn and head back to their house. Ronan sighs and scrubs his scruff, shaking his head.

"You think they did it?"

"No." He turns to face me. "But better me making them paranoid and keeping them out of the way than them going to see what happened to Chad themselves."

"Makes sense."

A few minutes pass in silence.

"What was your childhood like?" I ask, growing tired of the silence because my thoughts keep turning to Chad's mutilated body.

"My dad wasn't around much, because he left my mom for another woman and made a new family. I spent a lot of time with my grandma while my mom went on benders, but she was always reading romance books. And while she was nice, I was sort of left to fend for myself."

"Ah. That explains the hair. Fabio strikes again."

He scoffs. "Fabio was my hero."

"Whatever," I laugh and elbow him.

"I'm serious! My grandma had shelves of books with this beefy, long haired man. She and all her friends fawned over him and how he was a real man." He shakes his head. "I was young and impressionable, but I can't say they're wrong. You should've seen how women treated me once I turned eighteen and started getting muscles."

"Oh, I can imagine. To be fair, your hair is really nice."

"Thanks." He grins and reaches back to touch his man bun. "Is it weird that I miss him even though he forgot about me?"

"Of course not," I say, shaking my head.

His eyes drift off, processing whatever memory popped into his head.

I glance away, thinking about my own family while he loses himself in thoughts of home. I don't think it'll ever get easier, but somehow knowing how much he went through with his family makes me appreciate the time I had with my own even more.

Family is everything to me. Or at least, it was.

Someday, I'll get back to them. I have to believe that will happen, because otherwise, what's the point?

twenty-eight

BELLATRIX

When I see Dax and Creed walking with a man in cowboy boots, I know shit's about to get real. This must be the investigator. His tan cowboy hat sits atop a head full of curls, giving him a boyish appeal, but his eyes are laser focused. His appearance screams cop, and from all the way up here, I can still feel when the weight of his stare settles on me.

"He's staring at me," I breathe to Ronan, the words barely audible.

"He'll think better of starting shit if he wants to make it off the island in one piece," he whispers back.

"That kind of talk will make you a suspect." I frown. "I'm sure it's his job to consider all suspects and I was Chad's fated."

"He won't take you off this island."

My heart warms. "Thanks, Big Guy."

"Anything for you, Trix."

The weight in those words is much more grave than it should be for the short time we've known each other, but then again, broken souls bond best with other broken souls, right?

"Hey, Trix." Dax's voice carries to us. "Can you come down?"

With a reluctant sigh, I stand. Ronan is up a second after me and practically climbs over me to get down the ladder first. My feet hit the ground, and I cling to the last rung for a second, taking a steadying breath before walking to the street to meet the investigator. A warm breeze curls around me, carrying the scent of the water with it. The sun is high in the sky now, and the temperature has risen enough to make a bit of sweat pool at the small of my back. Or maybe the investigator's intense stare is doing that.

I didn't kill Chad, but it's clear he's not convinced. Creed nods at me in encouragement when I flick my gaze to meet his; his forehead is creased with concern so the gesture doesn't do much to reassure me.

"Hello." I wave, like a weirdo, and try not to grimace at my ridiculous impression of normal.

"Bellatrix, this is Investigator Wilson. Wilson, this is Trix." Dax gestures in my direction.

Awkwardly stepping forward, I extend my hand. The cowboy hat casts a small shadow across his face, but it's light enough to see the way his eyes slightly narrow before he reaches out and clamps his fingers around mine. You know those handshakes that are either limp and creepy or aggressive and startling? Wilson's grip is somewhere in between, intimidating enough to make me tighten my fingers slightly, but gentle enough to put me a little more at ease.

Calm and controlled. He studies my face for a second, withdrawing his hand before shooting his gaze around the guys.

"Dax tells me you were on a walk when you found the body?" he asks, voice raspy like he smoked a few too many cigarettes. With his outfit, I can almost picture him on the back of a horse riding off into the sunset while smoking.

"Yes."

Something I learned from getting into trouble when I was younger, don't give them more than they ask for. They want to make you talk, because they want to catch you in lies. I don't have any lies, but I'm not about to spill my guts to him and make myself seem more suspicious.

"And where were you last night?" No smile. Only a blank stare and expectations of me answering everything he might ask.

"I was with Creed."

"She stayed in my bed," he chimes in.

"Hmm." The investigator looks at Dax. "Where were you last night?"

"Sleeping," Dax says without flinching. "Ronan was on guard. Are we official suspects?"

"That's yet to be determined." Wilson pushes the brim of his hat, lifting it up a bit.

"Do you want to come to the house?" I ask, pointing down the road. "I'm burning up."

"If you don't mind." Another blink and almost bored look, if it weren't for the sharp focus of his eyes, I'd think he was only here out of obligation.

We get to the house and Dax goes to make coffee. Wilson, Creed, Ronan, and I sit in the living room. The guys on either side of me and the investigator in the recliner across from the couch.

"You all live together?"

"Yes." Again, no need to explain. Our living arrangement has nothing to do with a murder.

"And you're dating Creed?" He lifts an eyebrow, sliding his gaze to Ronan to check his reaction.

Nosy, perceptive bastard.

"Actually I'm sleeping with all of them, but I'm not sure what that has to do with the murder."

The edge of his mouth barely lifts, and he nods. "Just gathering facts, Bellatrix. So you were sleeping with Creed last night. Where was Chad?"

Sighing, I shake my head. "I don't know. Obviously by the dock at some point."

Dax brings in two mugs, grabs two more and sits down on the other recliner, turning it so he's facing Wilson.

"Would you say you're attached to her?" He directs this question to the men.

I press my lips together, wondering why he's questioning all of us at once. Don't these things usually happen one on one? I don't know if I want to hear their answer to this question. What if they're not attached and I am? Sex is one thing. Logically, I know we've all gotten close in a short amount of time, but attachment can mean something different to them than it does to me.

"Trix is family," Creed says.

"I thought you were sleeping with her. You have sex with your family?"

Now the investigator is being obtuse.

"Yeah, we're having sex with her, but our relationship isn't only about that. You've never been rejected, so you might not understand, but Trix fills in the void the rejected bond left inside of me. Sure, she's gorgeous and amazing in bed, but her heart and ridiculous sense of humor eases some of the pain."

"So you love her."

"No," Dax cuts in.

My heart stops beating until he says, "Not yet anyway. It's only been a month, so there are feelings that'll lead us all to love, but you have to understand, it takes time to heal and trust a person after being rejected."

The investigator looks at me. "You love them?"

I bite my lip, not wanting to hurt their feelings by saying no, but I'm in complete agreement with Dax. I don't love them. Yet.

"No."

Ronan and Creed's hands fall on my thigh, letting me know they're not upset. Sometimes taking care not to toss out the *I love you* phrase early on isn't so bad.

"But like Dax said, we're on the way to love." I smile at Dax. "I don't plan on leaving anytime soon."

He grins. "I'd drag you back if you tried to run away."

"You know that's creepy, right? I knew you were a stalker."

"Only for you," he shoots back.

The investigator clears his throat.

Crap.

"He's not a stalker," I say quickly, "we're joking."

"I do understand humor, but thank you for clarifying."

Wrinkling my nose, I hold his stare. "What else? I wish we had more."

"What about Harlow?"

I suck in a breath and glance at Dax.

"She makes the most sense," he says with a shrug. "And with the note…"

Oh. I forgot about that. Pulling it out and handing it to Wilson, I watch him read it, sucking in my cheek.

"Say it is Harlow. Why would she do this?"

Rubbing my eyebrow, I frown. "Chad tried to kidnap me. He didn't make it far, and Harlow came to the rescue in her wolf form. Between the two of us, we managed to delay him long enough for Dax to come."

"And what happened when you arrived?" The investigator leans back in the recliner, putting his hand over his mouth.

"I took care of things."

He's not impressed by Dax's vague answer. He rests his arm on the chair and leans toward him. "Meaning?"

"I kicked his ass."

Fighting off the smile that threatens to take hold, I glance at my lap and study my hands. It probably wouldn't be good to laugh right now. A few moments pass in a silence so absolute you could hear a hair fall to the carpeted floor.

"And Harlow, of all people, is the one who killed him? Because she felt bad someone she hardly knows almost got kidnapped by her fated mate?"

"When you say it like that, it sounds ridiculous." I cross my arms over my chest. "She's targeted two other men. Maybe she snapped."

"Hmm. That would be rather convenient."

"Listen," Dax growls, grinding his teeth together. "If you have something to say or ask, be direct."

God he's so cute when he's angry.

"Well, since you asked so nicely, I'll tell you what I think." Wilson cuts his eyes to me. "Sounds like you made some fast friends, and using your feminine wiles, you got these men, or one of them, to take care of Chad because you were mad he rejected you."

"Like fuck," Creed mutters.

"Yeah, nice try dude. If we were going to kill him, we wouldn't have left the body for you to find." Ronan scoffs.

"So how would you dispose of it?"

Ronan holds his hands up. "I'm not playing this game. You either need to officially charge us, or stop fucking around."

I grin without restraint. "It's okay, Ronan. The investigator knows we didn't do it, don't you?" I lean forward, searching his face. "But you knew that before we even got in the house, didn't you?"

He finally cracks a smile. "You think you know me?"

Shrugging, I sit back into Creed and Ronan's arms. "I think you're wasting a lot of time with us before you go follow your instincts, and I bet your instincts are telling you we're not the right suspects." Slowly arching an eyebrow, I harden my stare. "Am I wrong?"

I'm truly going out on a limb with this guess, because my intuition has only led me astray a few times.

"Only a little." He glances around the living room. "I figured you all weren't the suspects when Dax went to make coffee. You don't make coffee if you're guilty. Hell, you don't answer as many questions as you all did without asking for a pack lawyer."

Everyone relaxes a little at his confession.

"Be nice to her," I say, glancing at my hands. "She's not all bad."

Dax gives me a curious look.

"She helped me, and even if she did tell me to leave her house the first day, she didn't have to let me stay out of the rain to begin with, so she has a heart. It might be buried under a lot of pain and obviously mental issues, but she still has a heart underneath all of that."

"She killed three men." The investigator rubs his jaw. "Doesn't seem so good to me."

"One of which was not entirely unjustified, or at least, not to her. Chad was close to feral, demanding to talk to me or take me away from the guys. I think she wanted to protect me."

I chew on my bottom lip, studying the cowboy. He's big, maybe not as big as Dax, but he's definitely a strong shifter. On top of that, there's a gun at his waist which is most likely loaded with silver and behind that is one of those deadly tasers. I shudder, remembering what it felt like to have those high-powered currents of electricity racing through me.

"I'm not going to hurt her if that's what you're worried about." He taps the butt of his gun. "This is only in extreme cases. If she's reasonable and doesn't attack me, there will be no need."

"That's what I'm worried about," I mutter, glancing at Dax. "Maybe I should go talk to her first?"

"I don't know," he says, checking with the guys. They're tense beside me, clearly concerned.

"Harlow won't hurt me." How I know this with such certainty is beyond me, but if she wanted to harm me, she had plenty of opportunities.

She's a reject, like the rest of us, and she's probably hurting. While that pain doesn't justify her actions, she deserves a little compassion. Maybe a bit of understanding and a friendly face before the hawkeyed investigator struts up in his cowboy boots to arrest her.

Wilson clears his throat. "Perhaps it's not a bad idea. You can provide a distraction so I can get close enough to catch her if she tries to run."

I frown at the thought of him yanking his gun from his holster and shooting her, gunning her poor brokenhearted wolf down. She killed three people, so I know she has to face the consequences of those actions. It doesn't make it any easier though.

"Okay," I say with a nod. "I'll go first. Give me ten minutes with her?"

I'm not exactly in a position to make requests, but he dips his head at me, tipping his hat up.

"Tell her it'll be easier if she doesn't run."

twenty-nine

BELLATRIX

How is it that the walk to Harlow's home feels more shameful than any walk of shame I've ever done? Not that I ever felt particularly ashamed for a one-night stand, but there is a sliver of embarrassment that creeps in when you're strolling down a crowded street in a spandex dress and carrying your highheels in one hand. The countless shame-walks I've done have nothing on my Vans scuffing over the pavement, my feet carrying me toward Harlow's house despite my mind screaming at me to go back to the men.

Taking a steadying breath, I remind myself why I wanted to do this. Harlow deserves to know, I understand, if at least to make her feel less alone when they slap those silver bindings around her wrist and she's taken to the main island for her hearing.

Her house is my favorite in the cul-de-sac, more cottage like than beach house, and her porch is beautiful. I jog up the steps, pulling my shoulders back and lightly rapping on her door.

"Harlow? It's Bellatrix."

"What do you want?" she asks, voice filled with suspicion. I imagine her ducked down behind her couch, peeking over the top to see if I brought anyone with me.

No one else is here. Yet.

Grimacing, I press my fingertips to the door and drum them against the wood. "I want to talk, that's all."

"Where's the investigator?"

So she knows he's here. Does she know he's coming for her, or is that the guilt which comes with knowing she did something wrong making her worry about his whereabouts?

"With the guys," I say. "Will you let me in? I'd love some tea."

There are a few moments where I'm certain she's going to tell me to fuck off, but much to my surprise, her careful footsteps pad toward the door and she unlocks the deadbolt and the regular lock, opening the door. I smile at her, hoping she'll take my request for what it is, a genuine request for connection.

"I have chai, mint, and apple cinnamon." She steps aside and lets me in, scanning the porch before snapping the door closed and locking it. "Come on," she grouses, brushing past me into the kitchen.

Right, this isn't some friendly brunch. We hardly know each other, and aside from her magical vagina comments, she's barely revealed her true personality. I follow her, taking a seat at the counter and watching as she fills the teapot with water and sets it on the stove. She turns on a small radio on the counter, humming along with a song.

"Aren't you worried about electricity?"

She tips her head to the side and shakes her head. "I want to enjoy a real cup of tea and some music before I go."

I don't ask her where she's going, and she doesn't explain. We both know. She rummages around in the cupboard, grabbing two mugs, tea bags, and some cookies. The investigator only gave me ten minutes with her, so I'm not sure we'll be able to finish, but I don't want to make this harder for her by saying so.

"Are you okay?" I ask, studying her face which is growing paler by the second.

"No," she croaks, setting the cups aside and bracing her

hands on the counter, dropping her head. "I did—" she chokes on a sob, then tries to say it again but the words die in her throat.

"You don't have to say it," I say in a rush. "I understand what you're trying to say."

She shoots me a wide-eyed look, eyes filled with tears and pain. Her shoulders start to shake, so I slowly slide off the stool, hoping I don't startle her. I hold up my hands and approach her. Her eyes search my face, bouncing back and forth so quickly it almost looks like she's on drugs.

"You're okay." I open my arms, waiting for her to make the move.

A pitiful whimper escapes her lips, and she steps into my arms, finally letting herself cry. I don't know for sure what she's mourning, the loss of her old life, the loss of herself, or the loss of life she caused, but whatever it is, I hold her through it, ignoring how damp my shirt gets.

The tea kettle prepares to scream, but she doesn't move. I pat her back, trying to figure out what to say to make it better. If I'm honest, words never help. Words are full of potential disappointment. Actions are more than that though, so I wrap my arms around her a little tighter and simply let her fall apart.

When the high-pitched whistle fills the room, she sniffs and extracts herself from my hold, giving me a watery smile.

"Thanks," she whispers, then turns to finish fixing the tea.

She pours the hot water over the bags of tea and into the mug, filling them both before setting aside the kettle. I grab the cookies, and she carries the tea cups to the living room. We sit on the couch together, staring out of the big bay window while the tea steeps.

"You're not going to ask why?"

I glance at her. "Do you want to tell me why?"

She bites her cheek and shakes her head.

Shrugging, I lean forward and pull on the string of my teabag, bobbing it in the water. "Then no, I'm not going to ask."

Her swallow is audible, and she sniffs again. "Chad was a dick. He wasn't going to stop, trust me I know." She grinds her teeth together. "He. There's something." She sniffs and shakes her head, too overcome with emotion to say whatever she wants to say.

"It's okay, Harlow. I understand."

She drops her gaze to her hand and nods. "Thank you."

"They're going to make you think you're broken," I say, shifting on the cushion to face her. "You're not. Whatever your reason was for what you did is your reason. You don't have to be that person, though. There's therapists—"

Her bitter laugh cuts me off. "I'm feral, Bellatrix. They're going to put me down."

"I don't believe that." I shake my head. "You can heal, but you need someone to talk to, and a little kindness. We all know there's none to be found on Wolfsbane Island."

"You found some," she muses, biting into a cookie. "Those men want you as their mate."

I wrinkle my nose. "I don't know about that."

Scoffing, she jabs the cookie in my direction. "Don't take it for granted, not every reject gets a second chance at love, let alone a second chance at finding a mate."

Avoiding her scrutinizing gaze, I take the tea bag out of my cup, set it on the small saucer and take a sip, humming in appreciation.

"I thought I'd have more time," she says.

"Hmm?" I side-eye her, but see her gaze firmly fixed on the window.

No. Not on the window, on the cowboy walking toward her house.

"Did you hear me, Bellatrix?"

I look at her, noting how serious she is.

"Don't take it for granted. You have a second chance. Chad is gone. You can petition to leave the island."

"Harlow," I say, setting down my cup. "You didn't kill Chad to—"

"It doesn't matter why, remember? He's gone. You can be happy. He won't haunt you now." She drops her guard and gives me a true smile; it doesn't light up her eyes because she knows she's about to be arrested, but there's real happiness there. Happiness for me.

"Don't waste the opportunity." She shoves the rest of the cookie in her mouth, chewing it quickly before draining her tea.

I wince, because it's hot and has to hurt, but her healing will kick in eventually. Standing with her, we walk to the window to watch the investigator close the remaining fifty feet between himself and her house.

"You're not a bad person," I say. "You made bad decisions, but you can change."

She sighs, giving me a look. "Pot meet kettle. You're not bad or despicable, Bellatrix. Chad was a dick."

Laughing, I nod in agreement. "Yeah, he was."

A comfortable silence falls between us, and when the investigator stomps up the steps, eyes trained on us standing at the window, Harlow heads to the front door with far more poise than I would have. She doesn't beg for mercy, pretend she didn't do it, and she doesn't try to blame someone else.

"Ma'am," the investigator begins, but Harlow holds her hand up.

"I know who you are and why you're here. Let's get this over with." She holds her wrists toward him.

His eyebrows rise to his hairline, and he shoots me a look. I shrug, and he simply shakes his head and pulls out silver handcuffs, clamping them around her wrist. Harlow hisses in pain, and my fingers instinctually find the faint scarring on my own wrists.

"Bye, Harlow."

Glancing at me over her shoulder, she searches my face and nods, shuttering herself and thoughts. "Bye, Bellatrix."

≈

THE MOOD FOR THE NEXT FEW DAYS IS SUBDUED. WE STILL watch over the supplies, but with even less shifters than before. The remaining ones keep to themselves even though the murderer has been taken, and Dax loosens up his strict scheduling.

There are plenty of supplies to go around, and there were even before everything that happened, but I think he's finally come to terms with the fact that there's more to life here than his control over making sure the peace is kept. Besides, no amount of guard shifts stopped what Harlow did.

Dax and Creed are in the kitchen cooking lunch while I'm working on a puzzle. It's only five hundred pieces, but either I'm really stupid or they purposefully make these things hard because no matter how many times I try, I can't get the border done. Ronan went for a walk a little while ago, probably to get out of cooking, so I sit back and watch my men work.

Creed is adorable with his pink cheeks as Dax stands behind him, directing him on how to properly slice an onion (who knew there was a right and wrong way?). I notice Dax shift a little closer, taking a barely noticeable inhale, but Creed's movements slow, telling me he is all too aware of what Dax did.

"Easy, Old Man. Don't scare him," I tease, walking to the barstool and sitting in it.

Dax grins at me, but doesn't step back, crowding Creed's

space on purpose. He doesn't seem to mind though, and ever so slightly, he leans back against Dax, their bodies aligning almost perfectly. I sigh, tipping my head to the side and imagining them naked. They've waited a long time for this, even though Creed was blind to Dax's obvious attraction.

"I think he should be the one who is scared," Creed drawls, sliding his gaze in my direction. "We might break him."

"It *would* be a shame to break his hip," I murmur as a grin tugs at my lips. I hadn't expected him to be so willing to include me in what was happening between them, but I love that he wants me there and that neither seem to mind. Something about this feels so natural, almost like it was meant to be.

That's sappy talk, though, so I shove the thought aside and smirk at Dax.

"What do you say, Dax? Think you can handle the both of us?"

He grunts, wrapping his arm around Creed's stomach and resting his palm on his lower belly, tugging his body more firmly against his. "I think I can manage."

Groaning, Creed drops his head back against Dax's shoulder, gasping when Dax slips his hand beneath his jeans and grabs his dick.

"Fuck," he chokes out, jerking his hips forward.

Dax chuckles darkly, stroking him a second time before pulling his hand out of Creed's pants.

"Ask nicely."

"Touch me, please," Creed says, easily falling into the submissive role.

"Very good." Dax wraps his fingers around Creed's shaft, eyes lifting to meet mine. "Tell me what to do to him."

"Stroke him."

With a wicked grin, Dax languidly works Creed's cock,

backing off every time Creed makes a noise, edging him like he did me the other day. His teeth graze over Creed's neck, and I gasp when he clamps his mouth around his pulse point. Creed moans and rocks his hips forward, trying to find his release.

Fuck, this is so hot.

Dax glances at me, dropping a kiss where he bit Creed and withdrawing his hand before Creed can come. "We should go to my room."

Turning off the stove, he pins me with a domineering, expectant look. With a huff, I hop off the barstool and march up the stairs like a good girl. Creed races after me, scooping me into his arms and carrying me into Dax's room. He drops me on the bed and strips in two seconds flat.

Dax eases the door shut, resting his hands against the wood and watching as Creed helps me out of my own clothes. My heart is racing as fast as Creed's, but Dax's is a steady thrum of anticipation, sure and secure in what's about to happen.

Has he done this before?

Whatever, it doesn't matter.

"Creed, make her feel good." Dax's words leave no room for argument.

Crawling back on the bed, I open my thighs and slip my finger down between my folds, lifting my hips into the touch. Creed tsks, grabs my hand, and sucks my finger, lapping his tongue around and savoring the flavor.

"Greedy woman." His finger explores my folds, swirling over my clit and sliding toward my entrance but hesitating, drawing out the anticipation.

"Creed," I snap impatiently, and Dax does one of his husky laughs, making my spine tingle.

"Not yet," Dax commands, resting his head back and

tipping his chin up, gazing at me with hooded eyes. "See how much you can make her beg."

"With pleasure." Creed buries his face in my pussy, lapping, sucking, and tongue fucking me, bringing me closer to the edge but backing off each time I whimper and my thighs clench together, teasing me.

Edging me.

Fuckers.

I kind of love it though.

Also hate it given the fact that I haven't come yet and I'd very much like to.

"Touch yourself." Dax moves from the door, standing over the bed in mere seconds and leaning over me, hands placed on either side of my head. "Roll those pretty nipples between your fingers."

God he's hot when he gets demanding.

"Of course, Old Man." I bite back a smile, tipping my head and batting my eyelashes at him.

He narrows his eyes on me, silently promising to make me pay before dropping his gaze to where my hands brush over my breasts. I pinch the pebbled peaks, tugging and moaning when Creed sucks on my clit at the same time. I'm so close.

My vision starts to lose focus, so I close my eyes, gasping when a strong hand clamps around my throat.

"Open them."

I snap my eyelids open, gazing up at Dax and melting into his hold, loving how his rough touch can turn me into a puddle in a single breath.

"You're not going to come until I say so, do you under-stand me?" His fingers flex a little tighter, though not in a way where I fear for my life.

Some guys don't do the choke hold correctly, but Dax?

Dax is a master, and I'm his puppet, helpless on his strings and more than willing to let him play with me.

"Yes," I rasp, licking my lips.

"Do you want something?" he asks.

"Kiss me."

His lips kick up, but he nods and lowers his mouth to meet mine, lazily swiping his tongue over the seam of my lips before I open to him, letting him steal every whine and gasp as Creed continues to torture me with his tongue and fingers. He makes a come-hither motion, stroking that delicious spot deep inside of me, and I grab Dax's neck, digging my fingers into his skin.

"Please," I beg against his mouth. I'm so close, right there. All Creed has to do is work me a little faster for another few seconds and I'd float to the stars.

"No." Dax grabs my hands and extracts them from his neck, moving to his drawer and pulling out a small bottle of lube.

I frown for a second then remember this is about more than me. This is about them. Us. All of us together. Creed is oblivious, but Dax gives me a knowing grin, kissing me deeply before moving around to the end of the bed.

Slowing his motions when he registers Dax behind him, Creed pulls his swollen lips away from my pussy and gazes up at Dax. It's such a pretty picture. Me spread wide for them to enjoy, Creed's innocent, almost fragile expression, and Dax's dark, filthy irises receding as his pupils blow wide.

"Climb up the bed."

Creed's swallow is audible, so I open my arms to him, sliding down a bit when he begins to crawl on the mattress so we can all be in the right position. Dax nods his thanks to me before flicking open the bottle of lube.

"Did you save this ass for me?"

I suck in my cheeks and watch Creed's reaction. His face

turns scarlet, and he glances away from both of us. I lift my hand to cup his jaw and gently turn him to face me.

"It's okay, Creep. He just wants to know how gentle to be with you."

We wait for Creed to answer. He stares at me, a thousand thoughts flashing over his face, and I smile in encouragement. This is a big moment for him. He shouldn't be scared or have any hesitation. He has to want this.

～

CREED

Trix's eyes soften around the edges, and her kind smile is the only thing keeping me from racing out of the room. I want this. I sure as hell want Dax, but I've never been with another man. My fated was my best friend, but he promptly rejected me when we found out. She runs her hand over my jaw, ever so slightly tipping her head to the side.

There's nothing but acceptance. Willingness to do whatever I want. She won't hold it against me if I back out. I don't want to though. The only way this is happening is if she's here too. For some reason, Trix has become an anchor for me, and if she weren't here, I'd be lost.

Dax is waiting, looming behind me until I give him permission. His strong presence makes my skin tingle in awareness. I'm overly sensitive to his every move, his every breath, and his every heartbeat. Right now, his heart is racing.

He wants me. Trix was right, I completely missed it. I want this, so I tip my head to the side to glance at Dax.

"I've used plugs before, but I've never had sex like that," I confess.

There's no judgment on his face, he simply nods and steps closer, running his hand up my back.

"That's okay, I'll be gentle."

A shiver races at my spine, and Bellatrix sighs happily.

"Can I come now?"

The hope in her voice is comical. She won't be coming for a while.

"Get inside of her," Dax whispers into my ear, hot breath fanning across my skin.

Swallowing, I position myself over her and push the head of my cock into her. Trix moans *yes* and grabs for my hips. I tsk and capture her wrists, pinning them above her head as I slide all the way in.

"Fuck," I murmur, holding myself deep inside of her. Her walls pulse around me, and I rock a little, smirking when she takes a sharp breath.

She feels perfect. Like she was made for me. Rolling my hips and grinding against her, I wait for Dax's next command.

"Bring that ass up." His hands run over the insides of my thighs to cup my balls. They're gentle, and his touch is fire hot, making my hips jerk.

"Fuck. Yes." Trix gasps and tries to wrench her arms free, making both Dax and me chuckle.

"Patience, Little Savage. You'll need to roll over too."

Since our current positioning won't work for that, I slide out of her, taking maybe a little too much satisfaction from the whimper she releases at my absence.

"You heard the man. On your knees."

She rolls over, propping herself up on her forearms and lifting her ass into the air. I run my palm down her spine, positioning myself, but Dax grabs my arm and gently tugs me back so I'm closer to the edge of the bed. I scoot Trix with my hands on her hips then line up with her center, shoving into her with a hard thrust.

A soft moan of pleasure escapes her lips, but before I can say anything, Dax's fingers brush over the back of my arms.

"Now you bend over her, hold her with your arms."

Trusting him is second nature. We've known each other for a long time and I know he'll treat me right. So, I drape my front over her back, languidly thrusting into her and banding my arms around her like Dax told me to.

"Good boy," he murmurs.

The lid to the lube snips open, and I shiver when I hear the bottle squirt, bracing myself for his touch.

"Relax, Creed. I got you." Dax grabs my left hip with his hand to slow my movements, moving his lubed fingers to get me ready. He starts with one finger, and I hiss and jerk my hips, making Trix moan again without meaning to.

"Easy. You're doing so good," Dax says, working my virgin hole with two fingers, scissoring them to help prepare me to take him all in. I gasp when he slides a third finger in.

"Fuck," I whisper.

"Shh." Dax's fingers brush against something within me and stars burst across my vision, whatever he's done making me want more of his touch, more of that electric caress.

I've grown completely still, breathing through the new sensations as Trix works herself against my erection, using me like a tool. Dax removes his fingers, kissing my shoulder and tracing his lips up my neck, brushing them over my ear.

"You're going to need to breathe."

I nod, swallowing the lump in my throat. "Okay."

"You're doing so good," Trix says, slowing her own movements when Dax asks her to.

"Breathe," Dax says, placing his hand on my ass and spreading my cheeks. He lines his cock up with my ass, and I have a moment of panic wondering how the hell it will fit, but he shushes me. "All you need to do is breathe. Don't think about anything else but breathing."

Pressing my lips together, I count to four as I breathe in, biting back a gasp when he slowly pushes in.

"You're taking my cock like a champ," he praises me, gently working himself in and giving me a moment to adjust before he goes a little deeper. "Breathe," he says, reminding me of my job.

One. Two. Three. Four. I exhale, gasping when his cock spreads me.

"Oh my god," Trix says, rocking back slightly. "This is amazing."

"Damn," Dax groans the word. "So tight." Then he pushes in all the way, his thick shaft filling me up. I cling to Trix, panting around the newness that hurts but doesn't at the same time.

It feels so good, especially when Trix starts to swirl her hips, reminding me my own dick is stuck deep inside of her.

"We'll move together." Dax bites my neck, tugging on my skin and moving his hips enough I can feel him gliding slightly in and out.

Mimicking his thrusts, I try to focus on both of them at once, but it's hard as hell. Trix's hands fist the sheets, and her walls are pulsing around me. Before I can think about how to make her feel even better, Dax moves inside of me and makes my heart stop as stars burst across my vision.

Holy fuck.

This is amazing.

"Touch her pretty little clit," Dax commands before biting the other side of my neck.

Moaning, I move one of my hands to her apex and slip it between her folds, finding the little bundle of nerves. I pinch it, and she curses me, but I continue to work her and the cursing turns to moans as her entire body starts to tremble.

"You like having me inside of you?" Dax asks, running his

nose up the column of my neck and placing his palm at the base of my throat. "You like fucking her while I fuck you?"

"Yes," I rasp, thrusting into Trix when he thrusts into me.

"Keep time with me, but not too fast."

There's no asking from Dax.

He's one-hundred percent in control. Who am I to deny him?

Ever so slowly, he picks up his pace, moving a little more in and out of me, making me moan. But he tightens his hold on my neck, reminding me I have my own job to do.

"How does that feel?"

"Fucking perfect," I say, reveling in the warring sensation of filling someone and being filled.

Together, the three of us move as one. Trix rocks her hips back as I slam forward. Dax thrusts into me, punctuating the movement with a gentle but firm rock of his hips.

"Oh fuck," Trix gasps, swatting my hand away from her clit. "Oh fuck."

I grin and move my fingers back, knowing she's right there and I can help her. She may be extra sensitive, but as soon as my finger finds her clit again, she cries out.

"Creed, oh god."

Dax chuckles and he and I move together. The pressure from his cock presses deep inside of me, making my dick throb. Trix pants, slapping the mattress like she wants to tap out, but she moans "more." I follow Dax's steady thrusts, pounding into her like he does me, losing focus on everything except for her delicious pussy wrapped around my cock and Dax filling me to the brim and taking me.

"That ass is mine, you hear me?"

"Yessss," I draw out the word, gasping again when he squeezes my neck tighter.

"Come with me," he says, kissing my shoulder. "Come."

His words brush over my skin, and my balls tighten, hips

spasming and cock jerking inside of Trix as cum spurts out of me.

"Fuck. Yes." Dax rolls his hips one last time, dropping his hand to my hip and burying himself as deep as he can.

Grunting, I hold Trix in my arms, resting my cheek against her shoulder and panting as Dax finishes coming. Trix wiggles against me, moaning in appreciation when she feels my cum all over her.

"Tell me we can do that again," she whispers, laughing softly. "Please? I'm not ashamed to beg."

Dax pats my ass, gently extracting himself and drawing another moan from me in the process. "That's up to Creed."

Taking a steadying breath, I nod, cheek rubbing her skin. "Abso-fucking-lutely." I can feel his cum trickling from my ass, but I don't give a damn. I want his cum all over me, marking me with his scent.

"Good boy," Dax says a final time before going to the bathroom to clean up.

Trix's legs finally give out, and we collapse to the bed. I pull out of her and roll to the side, tugging her closer.

"Mm. I loved that," she says, snuggling in my arms. "Are you okay?" She searches my face, a line of concern wrinkling her forehead when I don't immediately respond.

"No." I pause, giving her a grave look. "I'm fucking amazing." I laugh, kissing her cheek when she scowls at me.

"Jerk! I got worried for a second."

Shaking my head, I close my eyes and hum. "Don't worry about me, Trixie. I'm in heaven."

She snorts. "Wait until you realize we're still stuck on this stupid island."

Not even that can tarnish my mood. I've never felt more alive.

Never felt more happy.

Never felt more like me.

thirty

BELLATRIX

Once we're all showered, we head back downstairs to find Ronan sitting at his desk playing solitaire. He glances up from his cards with a knowing grin, eyes floating over all of us.

"That sounded fun."

"Oh my god, Ronan. It was the best." I go and sit on his lap, linking my arms around his neck. "Creed did so good." I slide my gaze toward Creed, noticing his pink ears. "But, uh, anyway, how was your walk?"

"Nice save," Ronan says with a laugh. "It was nice. I heard a few patrol boats. There are more than usual... kind of makes me wonder if someone actually managed to escape?"

"One can only hope," I mutter, watching Dax go to finish our food.

Creed's eyes follow him, unabashedly filled with longing, and I sigh, resting my head against Ronan's shoulder.

You should petition to leave.

Harlow's words echo in my mind, and I chew on my cheek. Is it even possible? Would the elders really let us leave?

"What do you know about petitioning to leave?"

The guys all stop what they're doing, and their attention zeros in on me. Dax wrinkles his eyebrows together; Creed opens his mouth to say something but nothing comes out.

Ronan hums curiously, dropping his cards and wrapping his arms around me.

"Why, Bellatrix, do you want to leave with us?"

I roll my eyes. "That's beside the point. Do any of you know how to start the process?"

"We can talk to the guards… but you'd have to go through the entire process, and if they approve you, which is a big if, then it all depends on an alpha being willing to take you back." Dax scratches his chin and glances away.

"Take us back."

"Us?" Creed asks, eyebrows lifting in hope.

"Well, yeah. I'm not leaving without you guys. Who would give me orgasms?"

"Is that all we are to you? Just pieces of ass?" Ronan shakes his head and sniffs, pretending to cry.

"I mean, there is the food part to consider too. You guys also keep me fed, so you know, orgasms and food, check." I laugh when Dax shakes his head at me.

He can't keep the smile from taking over his face though. "You want to leave the island with us?"

"Why is this so hard to understand?" I pat Ronan's arm and stand. He reluctantly releases me and I head over to my silver fox.

"You guys are going to come with me, and we'll figure out the rest when the time comes."

His smile falls a little. "What if it doesn't work out?"

Shrugging, I put my hands on his shoulders and look him in the eyes. "Why waste time worrying about something that hasn't happened yet? We have to at least try."

"I'm in, but if you break my heart, I'll probably end up on the island again," Creed says.

I glance at him. "I have no intentions of breaking your heart, Creep."

Gripping my chin, Dax turns me to face him. "Good,

because like I said before, if you try to run, we'll only chase you."

So that statement should send off warning bells, right? I think my warning system is broken because all his words do is send a swoop of heat to my lower belly. As if knowing exactly where they hit me, he chuckles darkly.

"You're insatiable." He kisses me, not at all bothered by the fact that I am indeed a horny bitch.

Considering what got me here, I'll take insatiable over despicable any day.

TWO WEEKS, FOURTEEN ORGASMS, AND THREE BLOW JOBS later, we still haven't heard back from the High Pack. Turns out petitioning was easier than I thought. After we waved down a guard boat, all we had to do was tell them our intentions. We filled out some paperwork and the guards took it back with promises to turn them in.

I'm not sure if the processing time is normal or if the fact that we didn't have an alpha in mind who would take us caused the delay. None of us could pick one, and since Dax's fated mate is still with his old pack, he didn't want to put her through seeing him again. I'm sure she's happy now, and his presence will only bring up painful memories for the girl. So while that alpha was our most likely bet, we didn't pick him.

Walking with Ronan around the island has become a new daily ritual. The time may fluctuate because of his schedule, but this morning we're out before it starts to get too hot. We've just passed the docks when a boat heads toward it. I'd be lying if I said my heart didn't jump at the thought of news from the High Pack. I grab Ronan's hand and we sprint to meet the boat.

I skid to a stop when I see Investigator Wilson, cowboy

hat and all, and Dean together on the worn wooden dock. Ronan storms toward the shifter who was supposed to help us after the first murder, but Wilson whips out his gun and points it at him. Ronan stops mid-step, lifting his arms in the air.

"Hey!" I shout. "What are you doing?" Ignoring the smart part of my brain that tells me to stay back, I rush over and stop by his side, glaring at the investigator.

"Bellatrix." Wilson dips his head in hello. "I'm here to talk, but I need your man to stand down."

Crossing my arms, I scoff. "I'm not telling him to stand down." I point to Dean, or whatever his real name is. "That's the guard who didn't do shit to help us. He deserves an ass kicking if you ask me."

Wilson's lips twitch, and Dean bristles at his side.

The slight movement carries his scent to me, and despite the lack of gasoline, I recognize it. He's the one who came into the house when the guys were gone.

"You broke into our house, didn't you, Dean?"

"I don't know what you're talking about," he says in mock confusion. "Are these two feral?" he whispers to Wilson.

Turning his gaze on Dean, Wilson lifts an eyebrow. "Do they look feral to you?"

I side-eye Ronan, who in all honesty looks a little wild, but that's only because he's pissed. He has his wolf fully contained, so there's that at least.

"The bitch looks half-cocked. I wouldn't be surprised if she was helping that other one."

"The bitch," I mutter. "Excuse the fuck out of you, but who do you think you are? You were informed about two murders. Two of them. You didn't report them to the High Pack and now you're here trying to say we're crazy to save your own ass?" I shake my head and scowl at Wilson. "I swear, if you believe this crock of shit, I'll find a way to punch you, gun be damned."

Throwing his head back, Wilson lets out a full belly laugh. Dean's face scrunches in confusion, and I continue cursing both of them inside of my head.

"You're wild, Bellatrix, but I don't think you're feral. I also don't think you had anything to do with the murders."

I drop my arms and gape at him. "You don't?"

He cuts his gaze to Dean. "It took me a minute to figure out who Dean was, Chucky, but after I did some digging, I found out what your middle name was."

What the Chuck? Chucky—AKA the dick who didn't report the murder balks. "You can't be serious. They're crazy. You know how the rejects are."

"Like Harlow?" Wilson asks, squinting at the shifter. "Your fated mate?"

Oh snap.

Harlow was Chuck's fated mate? This is the asshole who rejected her?

Ugh. Why is it these men with dumb names have the audacity to reject people?

"I don't know what you're talking about," Chucky says, voice filling with trepidation. "Whatever that bitch said is a lie."

Wilson scoffs and points the gun at Chucky when he takes a step toward the boat. "Not so fast, Chucky. You're new to the guard, so you may not realize her file had a permanent notation of who rejected her. Do you want to tell me the High Pack made a mistake marking you down?"

Face paler than ever, Chucky's fingers ball into fists. "No."

Wilson nods. "Good. Then we should talk about why you enjoy killing rejects."

Ronan and I share a look, confused as hell. Wilson obviously knows way more than he initially let on, but the information is all inside his head, so the best I can do is piece things together and try to keep up with what he says.

"I didn't kill them. Harlow did that."

Tsking, Wilson steps toward him. "She told me you made her pick who died. Like some sort of fucked up game of roulette, only you were targeting people you didn't think the High Pack would care about."

"She's lying. You talked to her, she killed Chad. Clearly, she's the one who killed the others."

Even I don't believe the bastard, not with the way his eyes shoot to the side, like he can't lie and hold Wilson's knowing gaze at the same time. I'm no investigator, but I'm pretty sure Chucky is guilty.

"Tell me something, Chucky. Did it feel good to sneak up on the rejects and inject them with silver nitrate? Did it make you feel like more of a man?"

Chucky snarls at Wilson. "Why do you give a fuck about them anyway? They're nothing."

A growl tears from Ronan, and I grab his arm to keep him from running over and mauling Chucky.

"I care because it's my job, asshole." Wilson glances at me. "Chucky here has a history of violence, except he's never been caught. I didn't understand exactly how the pieces fit until I checked into his pack history. Apparently, he's left a trail of bodies behind him. He can't control himself it seems."

My brow furrows, and I grimace. "So Harlow didn't kill Chad?"

"No, she did that," Wilson says, sounding almost sad about it. "But Chucky here killed the others, didn't you?"

Chucky's eyes are glowing yellow, his wolf shining through now that the information is out in the open. His body vibrates with anger, and something about the way his face goes slack, like he's flipped a switch and every emotion drains from his face, gives me chills. This shithead is a killer through and through.

"He rejected Harlow so he'd be able to keep killing," I guess, glancing at Wilson to see if I'm right.

"That's what I'm thinking too."

My heart aches for her, because no one deserves to be rejected, especially not by a psychopath who only did it so he'd have access to rejects he could kill. He probably thought he'd have his pick of victims for the rest of his life. Stomach churning at the thought of how he made Harlow pick, and what else he might have done to her, I bite my cheek to keep from screaming at him.

I have a lot of pent up anger, and knowing what Chucky did has brought all of it to the surface. Freaking out on him won't help Wilson, so I silently seethe, watching Wilson grab for his cuffs.

At least he caught the bastard.

"You're not going to take me in." Chucky releases a crazed shout before rushing Wilson, shifting mid-run. His wolf is in the air, teeth bared and gleaming with saliva as he launches himself toward Wilson.

"Watch out!" I try to run to help, but Ronan stops me.

Two shots crack through the air. The wolf yelps, body thudding to the dock and blood spilling from the wounds. Wilson curses, dropping to his knees and feeling around for a pulse.

"Fuck," he mumbles. "Dammit."

"Is he dead?" I ask, shamelessly hoping so.

"Yeah." Wilson sets his hands on his knees, smearing blood on his dark wash jeans and taking off his cowboy hat, dropping his head. "I didn't bring him here to kill him." He glances over his shoulder, eyes willing us to believe him.

"He was going to attack you. No one will blame you for

that," I say, walking over with Ronan. We stop a few feet away from him and stare at Chucky's too-still body.

The Wolf Guard has special bullets loaded with silver. They're meant to kill, and it's jarring to see how efficiently they operate.

"Fuck," Wilson says again, sucking in his cheeks. "This did not go as planned."

"Trix! Ronan!" Dax's shout draws our attention to the trees. He and Creed are rushing over, followed closely by the remaining shifters on the island. It's the first time I've seen them all out at the same time, but gunshots are unusual given that there are no firearms on the island.

They stop at the end of the dock, scanning the scene, and Wilson's teeth grind together. He probably hates having such a big audience right after he's killed someone, even if it was in self-defense.

ONCE ANOTHER BOAT FULL OF GUARDS COMES AND TALKS TO Wilson about what happened and interview me and Ronan, they decide that Wilson's actions were justified. He gets off with having to go see the psychologist, but he's not in trouble. Knowing he was the one who snuck into the house gives me a strange sense of peace because the fear is over.

They put Chucky's body on that boat and leave. Wilson stares after them for a few moments before turning toward me and the guys. He takes off his cowboy hat, fingers playing with the rim of it. What happened with Chucky unsettled him, and it's nice to know that while he's trained to kill, he doesn't enjoy it.

"I had some good news to bring too." He releases a hard sigh, looking at all of us. "Your petition has been approved, pending the psychological analysis coming back as clean, you'll find yourself a new home with the Northwood pack."

"They found an alpha for us?" I ask, voice rising a few octaves. "Who?"

"His name is Killian. He was actually on an island for a while too. His mate, Legacy, has insisted with the High Pack that her pack take in anyone who wants to leave the islands."

The idea is ludicrous but there's no gleam of mirth in Wilson's gaze. He's not joking. Killian is an alpha who was on a reject island. And we get to leave. Well, we get to leave if we pass the psychological evaluation.

"Holy shit." I laugh, shaking my head and looking at the guys. "It worked."

"We can leave?" Creed asks in disbelief.

"Once you pass the evaluation," Wilson says, making sure to dampen our hope with the very real possibility that we could fail.

We won't though, I'm confident in our mental state. We're leaving Wolfsbane for good.

Thank fuck.

epilogue

BELLATRIX

"Dax! They're here," I say, pulling my head out from between the curtains and glancing over my shoulder. "They're early."

He's standing in the kitchen, watching the fried chicken cook on the gas stovetop. The dark stained cabinets behind him are freshly polished, and after a full day of cleaning, the house smells like citrus. The dining room table is set, with practical plates and silverware, nothing fancy or elegant, but nice enough on their own. He grabs a beer from the fridge, chuckling and taking a drink.

"Relax, Little Savage. Dinner will be ready in five."

Creed and Ronan beat me to the front door, but I elbow past them and run down the steps of our new cottage in the Northwood Pack territory. It's not big and ritzy like the one we lived in on Wolfsbane, but it's home and we're free. There are three bedrooms, two baths, a kitchen, and a sizable living room and dining room.

The psychological evaluations came back clean, and no more than a day later did we get to leave the island. Things have been a whirlwind of crazy. Between meeting the alpha and his mate, Legacy, and her other mates too—turns out I'm not the only one in love with sex and having a harem—and finding a home, jobs, and meeting all of our new packmates, there's hardly been time to breathe.

Pack Northwood is more welcoming than I anticipated,

which is a relief. For some reason, I expected to be shunned and ignored, but with the pack alpha being a former islander, the pack must be used to giving people second chances.

It's been exactly five days since we left the island, but it feels like a lifetime. I've been gone from my family for almost two months, so seeing Bella's grinning face pop up over the top of Dad's car door has me laughing and crying at the same time.

Mom and Dad are slower to get out, but Bella slams her door closed and sprints toward me. We collide in a mess of tears and limbs, tumbling to the ground and clinging to each other. Her tears soak my shirt.

"I missed you so much, Trix."

I hold her tighter, breathing in her familiar scent, and for the first time in a long time, everything feels right. "I missed you too, Sis."

"Really, girls? You're going to be covered in dirt." Mom shakes her head at us, and we get up, laughing and dusting each other off.

"Trixie," Dad whispers my name, too overcome with emotion to say much else.

"Hey, Dad." I wrap him in a hug, and my mom joins us. They don't cry as hard as Bella, but there are enough tears that I worry what the men must think.

When we've hugged long enough to get a little uncomfortable, I step out of their arms and look at the guys. Creed is leaning against the railing of the porch, a cheesy grin plastered on his face while he watches us. Ronan is more serious, but his lips are slightly quirked.

"Trix," Bella says. "Please tell me you're with both of them."

"I'm with all three."

She gasps.

My dad chokes on his own spit, and my mom slaps his back, snickering at his initial reaction.

Looking around for Dax, Bella lifts her eyebrows at me. "Where's the—" Dax comes out, running his hand over his black shirt to smooth the wrinkles. "Oh my god. You're such a bitch," she says with a laugh.

Smirking, I tip my head to the side and eye my men. "I know." Dax's scruff is neatly trimmed, sprinkled with gray, and his fresh haircut makes him look like a GQ model. Ronan's beard is a little shorter, but his hair is still long and in a man bun that would give Jason Momoa a run for his money. Creed is the cleanest cut of the three, but he's still gorgeous. He smooths his blond hair, green eyes finding me with a rueful grin cutting across his face.

"I need details." Bella fans her face.

"Not until after dinner," Mom chides. "Trix, introduce us to your mates."

Without missing a beat, I point to Creed. "This is Creep. He stalked me, but I fell in love at first sight." He scowls at my sarcasm, but I simply wink at him and continue, jerking my thumb toward Ronan. "Ronan. He thinks he's great at board games, but he sucks." Ronan scoffs, and I stick my tongue out at him. "And this is Daddy Dax."

Dax growls softly at me in warning, and I know my ass will be bright red later, but seeing the way his eyes darken makes the pain worth it. Besides, I know he'll also give me an epic orgasm, so I'm not complaining.

My dad chokes again, and my mom throws her head back, cackling at how red he turns. If he were any other level of shifter, he'd probably be livid, but as an omega, he can barely get himself together enough to meet their gazes.

The men smile at my parents as we come up the porch, and Dax steps toward my dad.

"It's nice to finally meet you. Trix has told us so much about you."

Dad's gaze drops to the ground, but he takes Dax's hand and nods. "Thanks for taking care of my girl."

"Of course. She's a handful, but we love her."

I roll my eyes, heart fluttering at the L word, and laugh. "Are you guys hungry? We have so much to catch up on."

"I'm starving," Bella says, wrapping her arms around my middle. "For details."

"All in good time, baby sister." I hug her tight and sigh, watching Dax show Mom and Dad inside. Creed and Ronan follow after them, offering to get them drinks or anything else they might need. Bella and I stay on the porch, staring at the strange picture of my mates and my parents.

Mates.

Yeah.

We've decided to make the plunge, but first I wanted to make sure they'd get along with my parents and sister. I wasn't too nervous, but family is everything to me.

After only a minute of interaction, I know it's meant to be.

These are my mates.

This is my happily ever after.

"Bitch," Bella whispers again. "I can't even find one mate."

I pat her head. "You'll find someone," I reassure her, because my sister is perfect. She's not a disaster like me.

I give it a year before she finds her fated or meets someone she'll take as a mate. Bella is everything I'm not, and that means she's going to get a happily ever after a helluva lot sooner than me.

In spite of everything I went through, I'm happy. Don't get me wrong, I wouldn't wish rejection on anyone, but if Chad hadn't rejected me, I wouldn't have found my men.

As if sensing my thoughts are on them, Dax, Ronan, and

Creed all look at me. Dax's mind is obviously on how he'll make me pay for the daddy comment later. Ronan's eyes are filled with nothing but affection, and Creed winks at me, biting his lip and flitting his gaze down my body.

Yeah. I'll take this happily ever after over my fated mate any day.

THE END.

AUTHOR'S NOTE

Hey! Thanks for reading despicable! Bellatrix and her guys were a lot of fun to write <3. If you enjoyed this book, consider checking out my complete Blood Mafia series (sneak peek on the next pages). I'll warn you though, Demi is crazy stabby and her vampires bite :) .

Join Rory's Tainted Readers on FaceBook and come hang out! I'd love to hear from you.

To stay updated on book news, make sure you subscribe to my newsletter on my website www.rorymiles.com. There's also a special Enchanted Magic novella being issued through there, so what are you waiting for? Come listen to me ramble <3.

ACKNOWLEDGMENTS

To my amazing team: thank you for all your help! This standalone was harder in some ways than a series because I had to make sure to do the relationships justice and keep the plot moving! Wrapping up a harem in one book is hard and you all helped me make sure this book rocked.

To all the readers: Thanks for reading! Don't let anyone shame you for who you are. Embrace your inner chaotic goddess and love loud, dream big, and follow your heart.

Thanks for everything.

Rory.

ALSO BY RORY MILES

Coming Spring 2022

Pretty Broken Things

Bad Moon Academy Series:

Dead Wolf Walking

Dead Wolf Falling

Dead Wolf Rising

The Complete Blood Mafia Series:

Blood Owed

Blood Taken

Blood Bound

Tainted Power Series:

Her Retribution

Her Reign

Her Resistance

ABOUT THE AUTHOR

Rory Miles is a fantasy/PNR romance author. She loves cats, memes, gifs, books, writing, her children and her husband. Especially when he makes fried chicken. She loves writing about romantic shenanigans and does her fair share of reading. Her all time favorite books are: #whychoose.

For new on more adventure filled romance, make sure to follow her on Facebook and Instagram.

Please don't forget to leave a review! Reviews are a huge help to authors and Rory loves to hear from readers.

Facebook Reader Group: Rory's Tainted Readers